BAD NIGHT
AT
DRY CREEK

BAD NIGHT AT DRY CREEK

Cameron Judd

G.K.HALL & CO.
Boston, Massachusetts
1990

Published in Large Print by arrangement with
Bantam Books, a division of Bantam
Doubleday Dell Publishing Group Inc.,
New York, New York.

G.K. Hall Large Print Book Series.

Set in 18 pt. Plantin.

Library of Congress Cataloging-in-Publication Data

Judd, Cameron.
    Bad night at Dry Creek / Cameron Judd.
       p. cm. — (G.K. Hall large print book series)
     ISBN 0-8161-5057-5 (large print)
     1. Large type books. I. Title.
  [PS3560.U337B3   1990]
  813′.54—dc20   90-40693

Chapter 1

Charley Hanna shivered in the chilly Colorado wind but refused to return to the house. Instead he paced about the yard, smoking, casting occasional glances over his shoulder toward the door, watching wispy chimney smoke rising black against the gray sky. He would have liked to sit by the fire where it was warm, but the old lady had never liked him to smoke in her house, and with the doctor there and the threat of death hanging so heavy inside those walls, it was more comfortable outside, even with the cold. At least a man could smoke.

He looked once more at the house and wondered if the old lady was all right. He tossed his cigarette down into the dirty snow and listened to the faint sizzling sound it made as he dug into his vest pocket for his tobacco pouch.

"The old lady," he muttered to himself. What way was that for a man to think of his own mother?

1

But that was how his father had always referred to her, and there had been no lack of love on his part. And Charley loved her too, and worried about her now that she was ailing. If Pa were alive, he wouldn't have stood seeing her so sick. He had been a strong public servant all his days, but when it came to Ma he had been weak as mush. A lot of men were like that, Charley mused. Look unflinching down the muzzle of a rifle and then wilt away around women. That's the way Pa had been, and that's the way Charley was.

Everyone thought Charley was like his pa in almost every way. After all, he had taken over the same job as town marshal here in Dry Creek. He walked with the same slump, wore the same pistol, and spoke with the same slow drawl.

It had been hard when Pa had passed on, but Charley had made it. At least Pa had died on his bed in a natural way, not choking out his life with a chest full of slugs like it might have been. Things were more civilized now than they had been in Pa's day.

Ma. How was she? What was taking that fool doctor so long? It was hard to believe she was sick; it had always seemed to Charley that she would live forever. But it had been two months now since she had even been out of bed, and every day she looked a bit weaker. Then last night something had happened—and now the doctor had been in there the longest time, and Charley half longed and half dreaded to see him come out.

Another cigarette fizzled out in the snow. Charley kicked up a piece of snow and frozen turf, then glanced once more toward the door. It opened and Charley's newest cigarette, not yet crimped shut, dropped from his fingers. Kathy Denning had come to the door.

"Kathy—is the doc . . ."

Dr. Eugene Hopkins came out of the door behind Kathy, pulling on his worn coat. He had worn that same coat as long as Charley had known him.

He didn't give Charley a chance to ask how Ma was doing.

"Charley, I've always been straight with all my patients and their families, and I won't change now. Your Ma is in a bad way, and I don't have high hopes for her."

"What's the matter with her?"

"Blood clot hit her brain. It's the same thing that killed your Pa."

Charley opened his mouth to speak, then realized suddenly there was really nothing to say. Dr. Hopkins coughed and sent out a white cloud of steam from his lips.

"Can you say how long she has, Doctor?" Kathy asked in a choked voice.

The old man grunted. "Only the Lord can say, girl. That's beyond anything an old country doctor can predict."

Charley thanked the doctor and moved up on the porch beside Kathy. The old medic wheezed out to his buggy, coughing loudly, his shoulders stooped. It took him a long time and a lot of effort to crawl up into the driver's seat. He clicked his tongue and jerked the lines, and the buggy clattered off on the frozen rock road.

"His cough is bad. I wouldn't be surprised if it was consumption," Kathy said.

Charley said nothing, but turned and entered the house. Kathy looked after him thoughtfully.

Sarah Redding pulled her shawl closer around her and stared out the window. The sky was gray, cold, and threatening. So far the snows had been meager, but it wouldn't be long until the first heavy snow blanketed the Rockies and the Dry Creek community. Sarah was grateful for the warmth of the cabin and the stock of firewood outside. She had prepared well for winter, carefully re-chinking the cracks in the wall, laying in supplies for the months ahead. When the big snows came she would be ready.

She looked around the cabin. It was lonesome, but she tried to ignore the feeling. She had learned to shove it aside, to lose it in the bustle of everyday business. It helped her to forget the emptiness since John died.

John . . . what a husband he had been, working hard, building a secure home for them, talking in anticipation of the family they would raise together. When he had died, crushed beneath a tree that was to provide winter fuel, she had almost given up hope. But there was no choice but to do the best she could. She hoped many times on her bed at night that John was proud of her.

The homestead seemed empty now without a man's hand at work on it. But she had a fierce pride in all she had accomplished and was determined she would make it.

Her attention was drawn suddenly to something down the road—a movement where it curved around the trees. A rider was slowly approaching, his horse's breath sending out double puffs of white mist. She felt apprehensive. There were few riders out this way; who could it be?

Her heart leapt suddenly. Maybe it was Charley Hanna! It looked like his horse. Her breath quickened and a smile played on her lips. Charley was the only man since John had died who excited her. Her hands fumbled at the knot of her apron, and she wondered where she had left her comb.

She glanced again out the window, and her heart fell. It wasn't Charley, but a stranger. She eyed him with suspicion. Into the yard he rode, but did not dismount.

She peeped around the curtain and frowned, then stepped back into the center of the cabin, unnerved. The stranger didn't call, nor dismount; instead he stared silently at the cabin. Nervously she reached above the cabinet against the wall and removed a small pistol. She checked it. It was loaded. Her hand felt cold against the bone handle.

He called out then, softly. Strange . . . something in his voice was not right. She looked out the window again. He was pale and trembling, and apparently not only from the cold.

She saw him slump over the saddle horn, then slide limply to the earth. One foot still hung in the stirrup; his horse stepped restlessly. She saw a stain of red on his side.

Sarah threw open the door. The cold air

struck her, chilling her through the thin fabric of her dress. She ran to the man's side, hesitated uncertainly, then loosened his bootheel from the stirrup. His leg fell deadweight to the dirt, and he groaned.

"Mister?"

He moaned again. Feeling she had to do something, anything, Sarah rolled him over on his back and looked into his face.

A rough growth of beard darkened his jaws, but he looked pallid and ill. Sarah realized suddenly that this man had been shot.

"Mister . . . can you hear me?"

His eyes opened, lined with pain, bloodshot. "I need help, lady."

"What can I do?" For some unaccountable reason Sarah felt she might cry.

"Help me inside . . . got to have water, rest. . . ."

"You'll have to stand. There's no way I can carry you."

He moaned and shut his eyes. "I can stand, if you'll help me."

Trembling with fear and cold, Sarah reached down and grasped his hand. He strained upward, groaning as he sat up, then weakly he struggled to his feet. Growing even paler, he leaned against his saddle for support.

"Can you make it?" Sarah asked.

"Yeah . . . just help me."

"Lean against my shoulder—careful."

Her fear forgotten now, covered over by concern for this man's welfare, she put her arm around his waist, supporting him as best she could, and led him toward the house. With several groans and winces of pain he struggled up onto the porch and through the door.

"This way, mister. You can lie down."

He leaned against her as they moved toward the bed in the corner. She tried to ease him down gently, but he went suddenly limp and collapsed. She lifted his legs onto the straw tick, then worked at removing his boots.

He breathed a little easier as he relaxed on the tick, but seemed to be fluctuating between consciousness and a swoon. She eyed his bloody shirt. It would have to come off, and the wound would surely need cleaning.

She picked up a pair of scissors and began snipping away at the clotted fabric. The man stirred and came back to consciousness.

"Much obliged, ma'am."

"What's your name?"

"Murphy. Willy Murphy." His voice was very strained.

Murphy. A familiar name, but she could attach no particular significance to it. "How did this happen to you?"

He smiled sardonically. "Let's just say I had a family disagreement."

She frowned. He was being cagey for a man who easily might be dead if not for her. She realized that this fellow could be on the wrong side of the law. She stopped snipping at the shirt.

"You better be straight with me. I don't have to keep you here, you know." She was surprised at her own boldness.

He smiled his strange little smile once more and nodded.

"I guess you're right. But I have to have your promise that . . ." He chuckled painfully. "It doesn't matter. I've had it anyway."

His words confused her, but she sensed that he was about to tell her something she wasn't sure she wanted to hear.

"Lady, I can't expect you to make no promise, but I'd be obliged if you didn't go to the law with what I tell you." He paused and looked at her expectantly. She said nothing, and he gave a little philosophical grunt and went on.

"The law's after me. I was in on a bank robbery in Denver a few weeks back."

Her nostrils flared. "Was it the law who did this to you?"

He laughed weakly at that. "No, lady. My brother did it. Can you believe it, my own brother!" He laughed again, even though it clearly hurt him.

"Why?"

"I took the money for myself. Never did learn to share when I was a little feller."

"Where is the money?" Sarah felt sudden embarrassment when he gave her a probing look. "I didn't mean—I don't want it for myself— Oh, blast you. I don't owe you any explanations!"

"No ma'am, you don't. You might have heard of my brother, Noah Murphy."

Her eyes widened. "You're one of the Murphy gang!"

He saw the fear in her. "Easy, lady . . . I ain't going to hurt you. I don't even have my gun anymore. Besides, I got nothing against you. I won't even blame you if you go to the law, though I hope you don't. It was Noah that shot me. Y'see, I took that cash from the Denver robbery and hid it

10

good, where nobody could find it. Noah didn't like that and proved it with this bullet. I barely got away from him. Thought I would die before I found someplace to rest. If it wasn't for you and your place here, I might be out there freezing to death right now."

"Glad I could help." The words were very uncertain.

"I ain't going to stay here long, lady. I'll be on my way long before Noah gets on my trail. I just need a little rest, and some food, if you can spare it."

"You need a doctor."

"'Fraid not, ma'am. Y'see, doctors ask questions, then they go to the law. I can't afford that—you understand?"

"I understand you'll die if you don't get that slug out of you."

"You just leave me to rest, ma'am. I'll be out of your way before sundown tomorrow."

"Dr. Hopkins is a good man—you can trust him."

"No." His tone frightened her this time.

She drew away. "All right, then. But if you die, you can't blame nobody but yourself."

"Oh, I don't know . . . seems to me that

ol' Noah had a little something to do with it." Within moments he was asleep.

Sarah cooked some broth and made hot coffee. When she woke Willy Murphy about an hour later he was hot with fever and could take only a little broth. The coffee he finished, then lay back once more into slumber.

It was dark outside, and the wind was howling. Sarah kept a fire burning. She sat at her window and stared out into the darkness, listening to Willy Murphy's fevered talk in his fitful sleep.

Fine flakes of snow swirled about, coming to rest on the frozen earth, settling on the woodpile. It might be sooner than she had expected that the first real blizzard came. When that happened, travel would be difficult. She might be stranded here in this house, alone with this wounded man, waiting for the sound of horses outside that would signal the arrival of Noah Murphy.

The sun had hardly risen the following morning when Sarah was on the road to Dry Creek. The decision had been made sometime after midnight. Willy Murphy was a criminal, a self-confessed bank robber, and she had no obligation to do anything other than provide him shelter until the law could take him to where he belonged. And in Dry

Creek that law was Charley Hanna. She would see him, tell him what had happened, and in the company of Dr. Hopkins he could come with her back to the cabin. She would get this outlaw out of her life before anything happened—particularly before Noah Murphy arrived.

The cold town of Dry Creek was stirring to life as she drove her wagon into the street. Smoke rose from every chimney, and she smelled the aroma of sizzling bacon and boiling coffee. Her stomach was empty, but she ignored the rumblings of it and made her way to the jailhouse.

What would Charley think, seeing her coming in so early? She wondered if he realized how he made her heart race whenever she saw him striding down the street. She was sure he had no corresponding thoughts about her. Charley seemed to be a man with little time for women and little interest in them. If he had a woman at all it was Katherine Denning, who cared for Charley's ailing mother. There had been occasions when Sarah had seen Katherine looking at Charley in a way that clearly showed how she admired him. It didn't seem that Charley had noticed those looks, but one day he surely would, and then he would be gone as far as Sarah was concerned.

She couldn't suppress a shiver of anticipation as she stepped onto the jailhouse porch and knocked on the door. When she heard the latch opening she smiled.

Her face fell when Bo Myers opened the door. The young deputy grinned at her through a scruffy beard. His teeth were yellow and had prominent gaps between them. A true man of the earth, this Bo Myers, and he smelled and looked the part. Sarah wondered how Charley could put up with him.

"Hello, Bo. Is Charley in?"

"Yep. Come on in, Miss Redding. Charley's over here eating breakfast."

Sarah stepped inside and Bo shut out the cold wind. Sarah smiled at Charley, who was rising from his chair behind the desk and wiping a trace of gravy from his mustache. She noticed that he looked weary and rather sad.

Chapter 2

Sarah smiled at Charley, feeling a bit awkward. Bo kept flashing his yellow, snaggletoothed grin.

14

"Hello, Sarah," Charley said. "Didn't expect to see you this morning."

"That breakfast smells good."

Charley fairly jumped toward the potbellied stove. "Well, here—have some bacon and coffee. Bo, fry up an egg or two for Sarah."

"That won't be necessary, thank you." She recalled Charley's mother was sick and asked about her.

"Ma ain't doing too good, Sarah. Dr. Hopkins don't expect her to live long. I'm worried about her."

"I'm so sorry. Mrs. Hanna has always meant a lot to everybody in Dry Creek. She'll get better—you'll see."

Charley smiled and Sarah felt warmth steal over her.

"Something wrong out your way, Sarah?"

"I've got some trouble, Charley. I hope you can help." Charley looked at her blankly, then with increasing concern as she outlined what had occurred. When she mentioned Noah Murphy, he exhaled sharply and frowned.

"I heard the Murphy brothers had been involved in that Denver bank robbery, but I had no idea they had come up this way. You say it was Noah who shot Willy?"

15

"That's what he said."

"How bad hurt is he?"

"It looks bad. That's why I want to get Dr. Hopkins to go along with us. I brought the wagon into town. I figure maybe we can ride Murphy back on that."

"Yeah—good idea. It's a good thing you came, Sarah. Men like Willy Murphy belong in a cell."

Charley rose from his chair and strapped on his gunbelt. He cut an impressive figure in her eyes, and with his gun at his hip, he appeared deadly and powerful. It was good to know that Dry Creek was under his protection. Sarah recalled seeing Charley's father when she was a girl; Charley was the very image of him. As she looked at Charley, Sarah's fears of the Murphy brothers diminished. With Charley Hanna along, she would be safe.

"Bo, you stay here and look out for things while I'm gone." Charley put on his hat.

"Dang, boss, nothing will happen around here. It never does. You might need help with Murphy. Let me go with you."

"No, Bo. There won't be trouble from nobody as hurt as Willy Murphy. We'll be back in no time."

Charley pulled on a heavy leather coat,

lined with fur that spilled out around the neck, and on his head he placed the battered, weathered old hat that had become so identified with him that most people saw it as an extension of him. He put his hand on Sarah's shoulder and escorted her out the door. She felt a thrill of warmth.

They found Dr. Hopkins sipping a cup of coffee beside a roaring fire in his office. He welcomed them in cordially, doing his best to silence the coughs that wracked his body at intervals.

"Coffee?" he offered.

"No thanks. We've got business."

"A man's been shot," Sarah explained.

Dr. Hopkins' eyes grew wide. "Hunting accident?"

"No. And it ain't just any man, either. It's Willy Murphy," Charley said.

Dr. Hopkins looked blankly at Charley. "Who?"

"Willy Murphy. One of the Murphy brothers—Noah's brother."

The doctor nodded understandingly. "Where?"

Sarah once again ran through her story. She had hardly finished before the physician was up, gathering items into his medical bag,

17

then reaching for his hat and coat on the wall pegs.

"I'll patch him up good enough so you can put him behind bars, Charley. If he's still alive."

Charley started to head for the stable to get his horse, then thought better of it. "I'll ride with you, Sarah." They went outside together.

Sarah welcomed the prospect of riding all the way back to the cabin next to Charley. He climbed onto the driver's seat and took the reins in his big, rugged hands. Sarah climbed up beside him, and Dr. Hopkins followed. Sarah took advantage of the fact that Dr. Hopkins' wide rump required a lot of room on the seat, and she sat as closely as possible to Charley. He pretended not to notice, but she suspected he did.

The wagon clattered down the street and out of town. At the other end of the street Kathy Denning stared coldly through a curtained window, watching unhappily as Sarah Redding sat snugly beside Charley. She released the curtain and turned back into the room.

Charley whistled as he drove the team, but Sarah could tell he was tense. About a half-mile out of town he began talking about the Murphy boys.

"Those two are a rough pair," he said. "Twin boys, both mean as snakes since they was little. Take after their daddy. Pa talked about old Jack Murphy a lot—Lead Jack, they called him. Laid claim to a quick gun and an ornery disposition. Pa never met him—said if he had it might have come to a shoot-out, Pa being a man of the law and all. Pa admitted Lead Jack was one gunfighter he wasn't sure he could beat. Lead Jack wound up on the end of a rope. That's exactly where Willy and Noah belong, too, Noah more than Willy, from what I hear. It's a shame there had to be two of them boys—double trouble, y'know."

"Do you think Willy will be a problem?" asked Dr. Hopkins.

"I doubt it. He's wounded, and Sarah said he didn't have a gun. To be honest, I think we might find him dead."

"It's likely. A wound like Sarah described can drain the life from a man. I've seen plenty in my day."

Both Sarah and Charley knew that Hopkins truly had. He had led a rough-and-tumble life amid the wildest mining towns and cattle camps throughout the region, patching up wounds, taking his pay in whiskey and chickens as often as in cash, and moving on from town to town like a drifter. It was only when age started putting rust on his joints that he finally settled down in Dry Creek. He had become a close friend of the Hanna family and almost everyone else in town.

The talk continued for the duration of the trip until they reached the bend of the road. Charley pulled the wagon to a stop barely out of sight of the house. Sarah looked at him expectantly.

"I'll go on in from here alone," he said. "If you hear me holler, bring the wagon on in," he said. Sarah nodded.

"I'll go in with you," Dr. Hopkins said.

"No. There wouldn't be much you could do without a gun. And I would rather have you here with Sarah."

Charley climbed down from the wagon seat and hitched up his trousers before striding toward the house. Sarah noted that he loosened his pistol in its holster.

The house was silent as Charley approached. No smoke came from the chimney. The place looked deserted. Charley nonetheless felt a keen sense of apprehension, and he continued with great caution. His boots made a crackling sound as they trod on the freezing snow coating the ground. Fresh snow was lightly falling, and the wind whistled around the eaves of the cabin.

Charley looked at the windows. Still no sign of life inside—no movement of the curtains or hint of a passing body in the darkness of the cabin interior. He reached the door. The cabin was as silent as death. Carefully he reached out to the latch and turned it gently.

The door opened onto a dark room. The last coals of the fireplace cast a faint red glow across the floor. Still no sound.

Charley stepped inside, drawing his pistol at the same time. He looked around the interior of the cabin, searching for Willy Murphy.

He was there, still in the bed. Charley frowned. Dead?

He walked over and looked down into the bearded face. There was still a hint of breath about Murphy, and a trace of color in his cheeks. He wasn't dead, but he didn't appear far from it.

Charley returned to the door and stuck his head outside.

"It's all right! C'mon in."

The wagon clattered up, Sarah at the

reins. She expertly pulled the wagon into the cabin yard, climbed quickly down, and darted to the door. Dr. Hopkins was a bit slower, having to pause midway down to quell a fit of coughing.

"Is he still alive?" Sarah looked at Charley with wide eyes, and it struck him that this was a very pretty young lady. Funny he had so seldom noticed it before.

"Yeah, but barely." Dr. Hopkins entered, still coughing. "Dr. Hopkins, I think you better take a look at him quick, or we'll lose him. Not that it would be much of a loss, mind you, but I wouldn't mind finding out where he hid that bank money."

Dr. Hopkins nodded. "Sarah, could you stir up a fire?"

"Of course." She picked up several small sticks from the pile of wood beside the fireplace and tossed them onto the hot coals. With an iron poker, she shifted the coals around until the wood caught fire, then laid larger pieces of wood atop the smaller ones. Within moments she had stirred up a roaring fire.

Hopkins was examining the wound in Murphy's side. The man was unconscious, but Charley noted his eyelids flutter as the doctor probed the ugly bullethole. He hoped the outlaw would come around so he could question him.

"That's a bad wound. That bullet has to come out now."

"Can he take it? He looks like much poking around in that wound might kill him."

"That it might. But I don't have any choice. If that bullet don't come out, he won't live to see sundown. Every time he moves it digs in a little deeper, does more damage. Sarah, boil some water. I need to sterilize my instruments. Wait! I think he's coming around."

Dr. Hopkins was right—Willy Murphy was moving a little, his mouth opening slightly, his eyelids squeezing tight as if with pain. Then he settled back, moaned, and relaxed. Charley thought for a moment he was drifting back deeper into a swoon, but the young outlaw's eyes slowly opened.

"Hello, son. I'm a doctor. I'm here to help you."

Murphy's eyes darted quickly to the doctor's face, staring in surprise at the old man. He then noticed Charley. The young man's eyes dropped to the badge on his vest. Slowly he smiled.

"She went and did it anyway," he said. "Went and got somebody."

23

"It's a good thing, too," Dr. Hopkins said. "You're on a straight course to a tombstone unless we do a little digging in you."

"Let me talk to him," Charley said.

"All right. But make it quick."

Charley sat down on the bedside and looked sternly at Murphy. He felt vaguely sorry for the young man, but he rarely wasted much sympathy on men known to be thieves and quite possibly murderers.

"I'm Charley Hanna, town marshal for Dry Creek. I know who you are and why you were shot. And I'll tell you straight, boy: It don't look like you'll hang around this world much longer. So how about you tell me where you hid that money so I can return it?"

Murphy laughed, though it obviously caused him pain. "I'll bet you want to return that money, law dog. I never saw a badge-toter yet that wouldn't do his best to cash in on the work of us honest robbers."

Charley's hand came down in a ringing slap across the young man's jaws. The doctor protested, but Charley silenced him with an uplifted hand.

"Listen, boy, I ain't going to waste time with you. I ought to shoot you like a wounded horse. Lord knows that's what you deserve."

"Charley—you keep on like that and you'll be half responsible for his death," Dr. Hopkins cut in.

"Frankly, I don't care. The world would do better without him. But I want to get that money back where it belongs."

Murphy's eyes went dull, and his lids closed. Charley scowled and stood. "All right, Dr. Hopkins. Go to work."

Dr. Hopkins sterilized his instruments and set to work. Charley went to the fireside, where Sarah stood.

He smiled. "I know what you're thinking —I was too rough on a man who probably is dying. Am I right?"

Sarah nodded.

"I'm sorry you had to see that. But I know the Murphy boys for what they are. They came close to killing a friend of mine a few years back. He was a homesteader on down the valley a ways, and all he was trying to do was keep them from his daughter. They shot him, almost killed him. What they did to the girl I couldn't say to a lady like you. You see why I did what I did?"

Sarah said nothing, but looked thought-ful. Charley went to the stove. Sarah had built a fire in it and coffee boiled on top. Charley helped himself to a cup.

Willy Murphy was moaning and crying as Dr. Hopkins relentlessly continued the operation. Experience had taught him such things were best dealt with quickly, for protracted pain was often as deadly as a bullet itself. This bullet was lodged deep, and he was certain vital organs had been damaged. Dr. Hopkins wasn't positive he was making things better by his digging.

Sarah wanted desperately to shut out Murphy's moans, but couldn't. She went to the window and looked outside. The snow was increasing, the flakes larger. The sky was a leaden gray, and the wind was up, whipping the falling flakes into swirling, intricate patterns before releasing them to blanket the earth. This was not to be a passing storm.

She stayed by the window even after the operation was over and the moans had ceased. Behind her Dr. Hopkins wiped the blood from his fingers on a scrap of cloth. Charley came to his side.

"Is he going to make it?"

The old man shook his head.

Charley glanced down at the face of Willy Murphy. Its color was almost entirely gone. Even a man with no medical knowledge could smell death hovering, waiting to descend.

"And he never told where the money was."

"Charley?" Sarah sounded frightened.

"Yeah?"

"Riders coming this way."

Charley stepped to the window. Outside, the swirling snow was a white curtain, making vision difficult, masking the road beyond. But through gaps in the storm Charley made out three horsemen approaching, their shoulders slumped and their hats pulled low against the wind and snow. Charley clenched his fists, for even through the storm he could recognize the lead rider. He had seen his picture many times, once in a photograph and other occasions on wanted posters.

"We got trouble. That's Noah Murphy out there."

Sarah put her hand on her mouth and Dr. Hopkins muttered something unintelligible.

Chapter 3

The riders stopped within twenty feet of the cabin, Noah Murphy in the middle. Slumped forward with forearm cocked

27

across his saddle horn, he was the image of cocky self-assurance.

"Willy boy! You can come out. We know you're here."

Charley cracked the door and called out through the opening, "Who are you? Ain't no Willy here!"

"We know he's in there, and we want him. Ain't none of your affair, friend. Send him out and we'll leave you alone."

"There ain't no Willy here, I tell you! Ain't nobody here but me and my brothers."

"Friend, there ain't nobody in there but you, a lady, and an old man. We been watching you a good while. We trailed Willy this far—and you'd best send him out."

"Noah Murphy, I'm Charley Hanna, marshal of Dry Creek. I'm giving you a chance to get away without trouble, but you're making me lose my patience. I've got five deputies in here with me. You got ten seconds to move your butt or take your weight in lead. I'm counting now—one . . . two . . ."

The men looked at each other and smiled.

". . . three . . . four . . . five . . . six . . ."

Charley's hand crept to his pistol and drew it quietly from its holster. Outside the smiles continued, but Charley detected a look of growing nervousness in the riders alongside Murphy.

". . . seven . . . eight . . ."

Charley crouched. He motioned for Sarah and the doctor to hide on the other side of the bed where Willy Murphy lay. They obeyed. Sarah was frightened but intrigued. What could Charley do against three armed riders?

Outside the smiles had faded, and hands were dropping toward gun butts.

". . . nine . . . *ten!*"

In tandem with the final count, Charley's pistol exploded in a burst of fire. One rider outside pitched backward out of the saddle, his throat shattered.

Noah Murphy whipped out a black Colt .44 and sent a shot toward the cabin door just as his surviving partner took a shot in the shoulder. The partner grunted and cursed, letting his pistol fall from his suddenly weakened hand.

"Let's move!" Noah sounded the cry like a battle call, wheeling his horse around and heading off toward the bend of the road to safety. "Your town will pay for this!" he shouted across his shoulder.

The wagon remained where Sarah had left it, but the frightened team hitched to it decided to move at precisely the moment Noah attempted his escape. The outlaw found his exit suddenly blocked.

Noah pulled his mount up short. His partner was forced backward suddenly, his horse rearing. With one hand still gripping his wounded arm, he crashed from the saddle to the earth. Noah's horse leapt over the prone man just as one of Charley's slugs knocked his hat off his head and into the wagon. Then Noah's fallen partner was up, racing for his own horse. The animal darted out of his reach, so the desperate man lunged for the pistol he had dropped. Charley fired. The man jerked once, twice, then stilled suddenly.

Noah was gone, but Charley took no chances. He stood a wary sentry duty at the window for five minutes, becoming at last convinced that the outlaw would not return. Only then did he reholster his pistol.

Sarah and Dr. Hopkins stood slowly, both shaken, Sarah far worse than the old man. It was the first time she had seen a gun battle; for the doctor it was merely the first time in several years. He sent a smile of admiration at the marshal.

"Good job, Charley. You just did your Pa proud."

"Thanks. You okay, Sarah?"

"I think so. Are they dead?"

"All but Noah Murphy. He made it out alive."

Hopkins let Willy Murphy's wrist drop limply from his grasp. "Here's one Murphy who didn't. This boy's dead."

The crowd gathered slowly around the wagon that drove into the snowy streets of Dry Creek. The curious people stared in silence at the three dead bodies in the back. Charley Hanna drove, Dr. Hopkins was on the other end of the seat, and between them was Sarah Redding, her shoulders straight and her expression blank.

By the time the wagon had reached the marshal's office the people were murmuring softly among themselves and mothers were holding their hands over the eyes of young children, trying to block from them the sight of the stiff, snow-dusted corpses in the back of the wagon.

Fred Colestone was the first to speak to the marshal, who had descended from the wagon seat and was helping Sarah follow after him.

"Who are they, Charley?"

"Don't know who two of 'em are. Skinny

one's Willy Murphy. The other two rode with his brother Noah."

"You saying you shot it out with the Murphy gang?"

The crowd shifted forward to gaze with new fascination upon the dead forms. Old May Wirt began to sway and lowly sing a hymn about crossing the river and what would I find beyond, O Lord.

"What happened, Charley?"

"Willy there got shot by his brother and wandered to Sarah's cabin. We went out to the cabin to patch him up and bring him in, but he didn't make it. Noah and two more showed up before we could get away. This is the result." He motioned toward the bodies.

"How'd you manage to hold off three of them?"

"I got lucky."

"Why would Noah shoot his own brother?"

Charley didn't answer that one. Instead he moved toward the office door, where Bo stood gaping at the dead men. "Bo, I got you a job. Go get Duncan to take care of the burying. No need for a funeral that I can see."

"Yessir, Mister Charley." Bo stepped

from the porch and moved toward the office to get Duncan, the town undertaker. He paused briefly by the wagon to cast a last ogling look at the dead forms, now turning a decidedly unattractive blue. Then he sauntered on down the snowy dirt road.

"C'mon, folks," Charley said. "Let's move on."

Slowly the crowd dispersed. Charley stood on the porch until the last man had gone out of sight, then he turned to enter the jailhouse, where Dr. Hopkins and Sarah were waiting. For many minutes the street was empty and silent.

Down the street Bo Myers emerged from the undertaker's establishment and headed back toward the jail. Again he paused at the wagon, stared at the bodies, then stepped up onto the porch and reached out for the door latch.

He stopped when Charley's voice reached him from inside the building.

"No one must know about Noah and that hidden money, you understand? There's folks hereabouts greedy enough to turn dishonest, maybe go out and do a little prospecting for that cash. That money belongs in Denver, and if there's any way to get it back there, I plan to do it. And Sarah, you'll need to stay here in town instead of back at your place. Noah probably figures all of us know where that cash is hidden. He probably doesn't know for sure that Willy's dead. I know those two with him weren't his whole gang. We're in a tight situation, folks. You heard Noah's threat."

There was a silence, finally broken by Dr. Hopkins. "You mean you think Noah Murphy might really do something?"

"I can't see it any other way. He wants that money, and here in Dry Creek are the only folks he believes can lead him to it."

"Charley, that scares me. I don't like to hear you talk like that."

"It scares me too, Sarah. But it's logical."

Outside Bo hugged his ear to the door, straining to hear more.

"You think it might come to violence?" Sarah said.

"Maybe."

"I think the folks here have a right to know. Their necks may be on the line, after all."

"I know, Dr. Hopkins. I'll tell them, too. If there's any hard feelings about it I want them directed at me, not you two."

"Charley, if I stay in town, where can I

live?" Sarah asked. "I don't have any money, so I can't rent a room like you do."

"There's an extra room at my mother's house. You can stay there. Kathy will be glad to have the company."

Sarah doubted that, but she held her tongue. Charley had scared her so much she was willing to spend time even with a woman she disliked if she could thus escape fearful days and nights in her own cabin, wondering when Noah Murphy would show up.

At that moment Bo chose to enter, deliberately making much noise to give the impression that he had just then walked across the street and onto the porch. He was greeted by three serious faces and silence. Muttering to Charley that the undertaker would take care of the dead outlaws momentarily, Bo retired to his small chamber off the side of the main office, smiling to himself, basking in the luxury of secret knowledge.

Dr. Hopkins rose. "I'm going over to check on your ma, Charley. I'll see Sarah over that way, if you got things to do here."

"I'll go with you. I need to explain to Kathy about Sarah staying with her. Let me get my hat."

They left, and Bo emerged from his room.

35

He walked to the side window and watched the trio move down the street toward the home of Charley's mother. The snow fell furiously now. The streets were blanketed with at least five inches of the stuff, and there was no sign of a letup.

Kathy was in the bedroom with Ma Hanna when the three entered. She came to the bedroom door, smiled at Charley and the doctor, and glared with scarcely concealed coldness at Sarah.

"Howdy, Kathy. How's Ma?"

"About the same. You going to take a look at her, Doctor?"

"Thought I would. Excuse me." He moved past her through the bedroom door, pulling it shut behind him.

Charley looked even more solemn than he normally had since his mother had taken sick, Kathy noted. And having Sarah alongside him like he did was making her terribly curious. Charley fidgeted, turning his hat in his hands.

"Kathy, there's something I got to tell you. There's three bodies down there at the office. We all may be in for a bit of trouble. Sit down, would you? This will take a few minutes to explain."

Kathy obeyed, her heart racing a little.

Something told her she wasn't going to like what Charley had to say.

Mabel Hanna's eyes had a dull luster, but deep in them Dr. Hopkins could see the light of rationality that still lived in the tired old brain. And he knew that she had fully understood what he had just told her.

"I felt you needed to know. It's been a secret that only we have shared for many years, and frankly I never expected any situation to arise that might make it necessary for Charley to know. But you understand now what might happen if he doesn't learn the truth, don't you?"

Mabel nodded—a barely perceptible movement, but still a nod. Dr. Hopkins noted it and squeezed her hand.

"I would be glad to tell him myself, if it would make you feel better. It's going to be hard for you to communicate with him. You give me the word and I'll tell him."

The old lady turned her eyes to the old doctor, and he smiled at her with a natural tenderness made all the more mellow by his age. Mabel's mouth twisted slightly, and the doctor knew that she, too, had smiled.

"Not . . . yet," she said, the words

scarcely understandable, yet clearly comprehended by the doctor.

Once more he squeezed her hand. "All right, Mabel. You give it some thought. I'll be by to check on you again soon. You rest now. Good-bye, Mabel."

He left her alone. She stared up at the ceiling for a long time, her dull eyes thoughtful, misted with tears. Then her right arm rose and reached across her chest, stretching toward the bedside table and the pad and pencil that set atop it. Only after great effort did she reach it.

Every muscle aching, she began to write in a scrawling, almost illegible hand.

Kathy discovered Mabel's dead body lying cold in the bed, a pencil gripped in her hand and papers scattered before her. Kathy had long dreaded this moment, but now that it had arrived she could feel no sorrow, no pain, nothing.

But she already suffered intense pain of another kind: a brand-new hatred for Charley Hanna. For she had seen, through the window of the front room, how Charley had held Sarah Redding in his arms in the falling snow, and drawn her close. Kathy had felt something die inside when she saw that.

Then had come a strangely soothing balm of hatred for Charley and Sarah, with whom, it seemed, she was going to have to share residence.

Kathy looked at Mabel's face and lifted the sheet gently over her. She picked up the papers one by one, arranging them in order, frowning at the rough script. She began to read.

At last she finished. She looked again at Mabel's body for a moment, then left and entered the empty main room of the house.

With an iron poker she stirred the fire into full blaze and tossed the pages into the flames.

Chapter 4

Bo Myers stood alone on the boardwalk, watching the beckoning glow from the Lodgepole Saloon, listening to the faint tinkling of piano music from the interior of the log building. The street was empty and white with snow, and there was nothing for him to do. Charley had told him to patrol, but he had circled the entire town three times without finding a thing out of order, and he had no inclination to circle it again.

And anyway, Freddy and Joe Phail had entered the saloon, and he was dying to join them. They had raised many a ruckus in Dry Creek, those two, and back before he had been deputized Bo had often been right in it with them. Now he was supposed to be respectable, the kind of young man folks could look up to and count on, but there were times when the old days beckoned and the desire for carousing became overwhelming. This was a cold night, windy, and nothing seemed more inviting than the idea of a good glass of red eye whiskey in the warmth of that saloon, old friends around. Bo looked across the street at the log building, yearning in his eyes, indecision in his heart.

Snorting low under his breath, he stepped from the boardwalk to the snowy street and began to stride toward the welcoming glow. But halfway there he stopped, then sighed with the kind of despair mustered only by those who are about to sacrifice vice to responsibility.

"Bo, you can't go in there," he muttered aloud. "Charley is counting on you to stay out here. You know what'll happen if you set foot in the Lodgepole."

And he did. He would sip one drink, then another, and at last be roaring drunk and useless as a deputy. He would let Charley down, and that was one thing he didn't want to do. Charley had taken plenty of ribbing for hiring Bo as a deputy in the first place; most folks thought Bo was a no-account with not one decent fiber. But Charley had believed in Bo, which had meant a lot to the young man. Only a time or two since he was deputized had Bo yielded to temptation and gotten drunk.

"No sir," he said once more. "Can't go in there. No sir."

He turned his back on the building and began walking down the middle of the street, whistling. He made it almost a hundred feet before he stopped, twisted his lip, and turned and walked straight toward the Lodgepole. His anger at himself grew with every step, but suddenly disappeared as he pushed open the door and stepped into the warm saloon.

There were lamps everywhere. The music was loud, drowning out Bo's thoughts of self-condemnation. He grinned and tipped back his slouch hat. He would have one drink—one little drink—and then he would return to his duty. After all, every working man needed a break, and who knows, maybe something would happen in the saloon that needed the attention of the law.

"Bo! Ol' Bo Myers! Come over here and have a drink! Or do you deputy types not drink liquor?"

Bo grinned, then let the grin fade, for he recognized mockery in Joe Phail's tone. Joe found it remarkably funny that his old drinking and fighting partner was now a deputy and he took advantage of every opportunity to make biting comments on the subject. It irritated Bo to no end, but tonight he would put up with it. He wanted that drink too bad to turn away now.

"I reckon I'll have a drink if I want one," he retorted. But Joe grinned all the harder and glanced at his brother. Bo was in true form tonight and would provide a good deal of entertainment.

Bo sat down beside Joe, snapping his fingers at the bartender. He was determined to act unruffled no matter what ridicule Joe and his brother threw at him. "What'ya want, Bo?" the bartender called.

"Whiskey. A good shot of it, too."

Freddy Phail chimed in. "Now, Bo, you think you ought to be drinking on duty? Ol' Charley might not think too highly of that."

"What do I care what Charley thinks? He

don't own me, does he?" Bo stood and swaggered over to the bar to take his drink. Pausing uncertainly, he took the bottle, too.

He plopped back down in his chair and took a sip of the strong liquor. He almost choked on the fiery drink but managed to squelch his cough.

"Yes sir," he said. "I don't worry about ol' Charley. Ain't nobody got a hold on Bo Myers. Nobody at all."

"That ain't what I hear, Bo. I hear you jump when Charley whistles. Hear he's got a ring through your nose."

Bo looked up sharply at Joe. Bo's was a weak intellect. Lacking looks as well, all he had was pride. Any man who touched that prodded his most sensitive nerve.

"Shut up, Joe. I'll bust your head."

Rand Cantrell turned at the bar, a faint smile on his handsome face. He was tall, lean, dressed in a sharp suit and cocky hat, and it was the name of Charley Hanna that had drawn his attention. Anything to do with Charley Hanna could get Rand Cantrell's attention almost anytime.

"Bo, was it you who got Willy Murphy? I hear ol' Charley managed to do that without any help from you at all!" Joe teased.

"If I had been there, there'd be Noah dead

43

beside him. Both you boys know I ain't no slouch with a gun."

Bo refilled his glass and drained the whiskey in a swallow. It was starting to feel good in his gut, and the old craving was growing with every second. He had never been one to stop with one drink—or even three or four.

"That may be so, Bo, but I notice when there's any lawing to be done Charley leaves you while he goes out and does it hisself. How do you account for that, Bo?"

Bo was starting to get mad now. He tossed down another drink. His brain was being dulled by the powerful liquor. Rand Cantrell looked on, sipping his drink casually. The loud young deputy was amusing to him; the topic of conversation was not. The saloon owner didn't even like to think about Charley Hanna, much less hear about him. But he enjoyed seeing Charley's only deputy getting drunk on duty.

"I'm every bit as good as Charley Hanna —every bit as good. Charley might think he's better, but ol' Bo knows a lot more than he thinks. Yes sir, I know a lot he don't have no idea I do."

Bo threw down another drink, not seeing the new light of interest in Rand's eyes. Indeed, he had not noticed the man at all. Nor had he any idea that his words were increasingly hostile toward Charley. He was talking under the influence of the whiskey now, concerned with nothing but saving face before the mischievously grinning brothers across the table from him. Neither of them really cared what Bo thought of Charley, or vice versa; their only interest was in goading Bo further for the sake of watching him stew. But not so Rand. He wondered if the young deputy might really hold information to put Charley in a bad light.

Rand had not always hated Charley Hanna. There had been a time he might have liked the man. But that was before the marshal had humiliated him before a crowd.

Rand was a gambler, and a good one. But the same deceptive smoothness which made him a winner at the gambling table also had a way of making him enemies. It had only been a few months before that a young drifter had felt the sting of Rand's gambling skill, and like many other hotheads before him, he had sought to even the score with a gun. Charley had intervened to keep Rand from beating the young drifter to death after the gambler had kicked the pistol from the young man's hand. Charley had entered the fight, striking down Rand right before his own saloon patrons, humiliating him. Rand had tried to restore his dethroned pride by ripping into Charley like a wildcat, but the marshal had beaten him off with ease, even smiling while he did it, as if Rand were something funny, something worthy only of contempt. That had been more than the arrogant gambler could stand, and he had tucked the injury away in his mind, letting it fester and torment him, making him long for revenge against Charley Hanna.

He poured himself another drink and watched the Phail brothers continue their sport with the drunken deputy. For an hour they pumped Bo full of liquor and baited him with talk of how Charley was so superior to him, how Bo danced like a puppet when the marshal tugged the string, how everyone in town laughed about Bo behind his back and marveled he would let himself be so continually belittled by Charley.

Bo at first tried to defend himself, and when the thought struck him, Charley also —but at last he stopped talking and started listening. He was now fully drunk. All thoughts of returning to duty were gone. It never crossed his mind that the Phail boys might be lying to him just to goad him on.

The more they drilled their propaganda, the more convinced he was of its truth. He sat glowering, sipping his drink slowly now, wondering how he could have been such a fool as to trust Charley.

The Phails finally grew tired of their game, for clearly Bo was no longer going to respond. They donned their ragged hats and dirty coats and stepped out into the night. Rand stood in silence at the bar, studying Bo, who was seated now with his head cast down. Smiling to himself, Rand went over to the table, a fresh bottle of whiskey in his hand.

"Mind if I sit down, Bo?"

Bo didn't look up, but gestured toward an empty chair. Rand sat, deliberately scooting the bottle in front of Bo.

"Drink?"

Bo looked up. "I believe I will."

Rand sipped his whiskey, studying Bo over his shot glass. His instincts told him this young man might provide a key to revenge on Charley Hanna. And Rand made much of his living trusting his instincts.

"Bo, I heard the Phail brothers giving you a hard time just now. Didn't seem right to me. I bet you know a good deal more about

47

this town and Charley Hanna than you let on. I've always thought that."

Bo looked at the gambler, smiling. After the bruising his ego had taken he was ready to hear anything that sounded like praise.

"You got it right, Mr. Cantrell. Charley would be surprised to find out what I know about him. Plenty surprised."

"I'd say he would. Here—more whiskey. It's a cold night. You'll need it."

"Thanks a lot, Mr. Cantrell. It is a mite cold."

Rand leaned back and watched Bo drain the drink.

"Yes sir, Bo, I wouldn't be surprised if you knew a lot of secrets about Charley— things he might not want spread around. Living right there in that office like you do, why, I bet you find out a lot of things."

Bo grinned, his bloodshot eyes shining. "You got it, Mr. Cantrell. Ol' Charley's secrets ain't as secret as he thinks they are. Not a bit."

Rand took on a more skeptical look that did not go unnoticed by Bo.

"Sure, you know things, Bo, but do you know important things?"

"Yes sir, I know important things—real important things."

Rand leaned forward. "Like what?"

Bo licked his lips and looked around. He too leaned forward and spoke in a low voice.

"Like how Charley was talking to Sarah Redding and Dr. Hopkins about Murphy money hid out in the woods somewhere, and about how Noah Murphy would be riding in to find out where it was. I heard 'em talking just a little after they come in with Willy Murphy. Yes sir, I heard it all myself."

Rand leaned back. "You don't say! You *do* know something important, Bo. More important than you might realize. Here—take the bottle. You and I need to have a good talk, a good long talk."

Bo grinned at his companion and felt that he had won. He liked it when people paid attention to him and talked as if he was important. Right now he would say anything to keep Rand's attention focused on him. He tipped the bottle and strong whiskey flowed again into his glass. If Rand wanted talk, he would get it—plenty of it.

Chapter 5

The skies cleared a little the following day, and for that Charley was glad. It would have

49

been hard enough to carry his mother to her burial place under the best circumstances, and cloudy skies would only have made it worse. The wind was cold and the crowd of mourners huddled closely together as they trudged up a small hillside marked with rude wooden crosses, hand-engraved tombstones, and an occasional store-bought monument that had been lugged by supply wagon from Denver. It was a quiet and somber place, and with the white blanket of snow over all, the dark grave dug for Mabel Hanna reminded Charley of a gaping mouth. Charley felt he should be crying, but he couldn't.

Virtually the whole town was there, including those who were friends of Charley and those who had cause to hate him. Weddings and funerals always drew a crowd in Dry Creek, for there were few sources of diversion for the townsfolk. But Mabel Hanna would have had no lack of mourners anyway; she had been a woman loved by almost everyone, even those who hated Charley and his father. Even Rand Cantrell, who lingered toward the rear of the crowd, recognized she had been a good woman.

Charley had noticed Rand among the mourners and was rather surprised the man had shown up. He knew Rand had no love for him—though he was in no way suspicious that the man loathed him as much as he truly did—and he couldn't see why the gambler would suffer the cold wind to see the mother of a man he disliked laid to rest. But Charley did no more than casually ponder the mystery; his grief had evicted other considerations from his mind.

Though not entirely. In the back of his mind he thought constantly of Noah Murphy and felt the dread of possible trouble hanging like a suspended blade over his head. He had realized from the moment the burial service was called that this would be the perfect opportunity to tell the people of Dry Creek about Noah's threat, and he intended to do so as soon as his mother was properly laid beneath the frozen earth. Then preparations could be made for defense against a possible attack.

Preacher Bartlett looked appropriately solemn as he waited for the mourners to quit stirring about before he began his eulogy. The coffin, a crude pine box, had been placed beside the open grave, ropes beneath it by which it could be lowered into the hole. The pallbearers were ruddy-faced in the cold and puffed a bit from the exertion of carrying the coffin up the steep, rough slope to the graveyard.

Charley stood beside Kathy, whose eyes were red and moist. She seemed quite disturbed, but no one thought it unusual. After all, she had nursed Mabel for years. It was to be expected that the woman's death would bother her very much. Sarah noticed that Kathy repeatedly cast glances toward Charley, who himself took no apparent notice of the fleeting looks. Charley looked weary and almost old in the feeble sunlight; many in the crowd noticed again the remarkable resemblance he bore to his late father, who lay buried beneath the snow beside the fresh grave that would in minutes receive the body of Mabel.

"Friends and neighbors, we are gathered to perform the sad duty of returning the body of Mabel Hanna to the soil from which it came," began the preacher. "Truly it is a sad duty on this earthly side, for we have all known and loved Mabel throughout the years, but let it give us peace to know that even now the angels are rejoicing on that distant shore to welcome the one who has come into their midst. While we moan and cry over our loss, truly the Kingdom of God sings in joy at its gain, and while we stand

and shiver in the cold wind of these Colorado mountains, surely our friend Mabel does stand and enjoy the warmth of the sweet wind that blows across Jordan from the everlasting hills of that blessed land which we all seek. . . ."

Already Charley had let his attention drop away from what the preacher was saying, for he had heard it all before, at other funerals. Preacher Bartlett usually said the same things. Through Charley's mind was running a cycle of images, vivid pictures of times past, when he was young and his mother and father were with him. He remembered their faces unlined by the wrinkles of age, free of the weariness of being old, and the memory made him happy and sad at the same time. He lifted his eyes and studied the clouds floating on the horizon, far above the sharp, snowy peaks of the mountains that loomed majestically around the burial place and the crowd of people. He found himself wishing, as he had many times in youth, that he could escape from the drab, mundane life of this small town. The preacher's voice droned on, the words not registering in Charley's mind.

Dr. Hopkins was staring not at the mountains but at the coffin. Occasionally he would cough, and his frame would be jolted.

The last prayer was said and the pall-bearers moved to the sides of the coffin. Slowly the coffin was lowered into the hole, creaking and popping while the men holding the ropes puffed and grunted with their burden. A few ladies of the group struck up a feeble hymn, the music whipping away in the wind as they sang. Charley watched the box descend and his heart felt like lead.

When the box was lowered Charley did what was expected of him: He took a shovel, scooped up a bit of dirt, and dropped it onto the coffin. It made a hollow, dull sound.

Then it was over. Mabel's funeral was done. She was left to lie silently beside her husband.

But it wasn't over for Charley. The thing he had to tell the crowd came back to mind, and he was struck with dread. How would the people react?

He started to speak, but before he could, he noticed that all eyes had turned to Rand Cantrell, who had climbed up onto a stump, his hands raised to draw the attention of the crowd.

Bo Myers' voice came to him from behind Charley, a cracked, hoarse whisper: "Oh, no." Charley turned to the young deputy. Bo's face was very white.

"Bo, what's wrong?"

There was no time for Bo to answer, for Rand began to speak in a clear, loud voice.

"Friends . . . friends, stop for a moment. I have something to say that all of you should hear. It isn't good, and I know that perhaps so sacred a time as a funeral is not the best time to bring bad news, but I have no choice. Please, don't leave . . . listen. You all need the information I have. It has to do with our own marshal Charley Hanna, some stolen money hidden by the Noah Murphy gang, and possible danger to our town."

Many faces had evidenced initial irritation at seeing a saloon owner and professional gambler drawing attention to himself at the funeral of so respected a lady as Mabel Hanna. But now irritation changed to interest. The movement of the crowd ceased.

"What are you talking about, Rand?" someone asked.

"I'm talking about a violation of trust, and a marshal who has deliberately withheld important information from all of us in order to better his own position.

"I talked last night to Deputy Bo Myers, and what he had to say bothered me. Deputy Myers overheard Charley, Sarah Redding, and Dr. Hopkins talking in the marshal's office immediately after the bodies of Willy Murphy and his two companions were brought in. Charley was talking about money hidden by Willy Murphy, money that his brother Noah wants. Bo heard Charley tell the others to say nothing about the money to any of us, even though the marshal said Noah Murphy threatened to make some sort of attack upon Dry Creek.

"You see, apparently Murphy is convinced our marshal and his friends know where that money is hidden. He believes that Willy Murphy revealed that information before he died. And from the secretive way in which the marshal was acting, I suspect Murphy is right.

"It appears Charley Hanna has some explaining to do. Can you deny what I've said, Charley?"

Bo cut in before Charley could answer. "He's twisting what I said, Charley. I never meant to—"

"Let the marshal answer," Rand interrupted.

Rage jolted through Charley, for Rand Cantrell had placed him in a position from which there was no good escape. If he said Rand was right about the hidden money, it would look as if Charley truly had intended to keep the affair a secret. To say he had been about to speak when Rand cut in would not sound convincing, even though it was true. And to deny what Rand said would be equivalent to leaving the town undefended from attack by the Murphy gang, should such a thing actually occur. And so for a moment Charley stammered, and that in itself only lent credibility to Rand Cantrell's statement.

"We're waiting, Marshal."

"You've told a bunch of half-truths, Rand. It is true that Willy Murphy talked about hidden money, but he never said where it was. And I had no plans to keep the thing a secret. I would have spoken up just a moment ago if you hadn't jumped up on that stump. And whether Noah Murphy will attack Dry Creek I can't say—that's just speculation. He did make a threat. But I did not intend to leave the town in the dark about it, and I had no plans for trying to find and keep that money for myself. And if I did find it I would just take it back to Denver where it belongs."

"Come now, Marshal. If you were going to tell the town about it, why didn't you do so when you brought the bodies in? You had a good chance. Plenty of people were standing 'round looking at the bodies in the wagon."

Charley did not respond because he had no good answer. He had hardly had a chance to think the situation through when he brought in the bodies, and the idea of informing the town then simply had not crossed his mind. Now that oversight was making him look quite bad.

"Do you really think Noah Murphy would attack a town?" someone asked.

"I hope not," Charley responded. "But Noah Murphy ain't the kind to give in easy when something is taken from him. He might attack us, if he thinks he can gain from it."

The marshal looked around at the encircling faces. He saw expressions of suspicion, doubt, and fear. In spite of his history of honesty and fair dealings with the townsfolk, it was clear that Rand's venom had taken effect. A seed of doubt had been sown.

The crowd began to disperse, moving on down the hillside. Charley watched them leave. He looked at Rand and felt a surge of bitterness. The gambler had twisted the truth just enough to put Charley into a pinch from which he would not wriggle free.

Sarah came to him. "Some of them may

doubt you, Charley, but most will stick with you. You'll see."

"I just hope the town has enough sense to prepare for attack. I'm afraid some will get it into their heads to look for that money. With Noah Murphy around, that could be deadly. Maybe that's part of the reason I hesitated in telling them about it all. But somehow even that wouldn't have sounded right if I had tried to say it. It would only look like I didn't want anybody else to know about that cash."

Bo Myers stood off from Charley, shaken and ashamed, realizing what his indiscretion of the night before had done. He had told everything he knew to Rand, filling in the gaps with his own imagination. And Rand had taken that distorted picture of the facts and cleverly used it to good effect against Charley. Bo felt now he wouldn't be worth the bullet it would take to shoot himself.

The deputy glanced at Kathy, who stood on the edge of the dispersing crowd. She was watching Charley slip his arm around the waist of Sarah Redding, and even in his distraught state Bo noticed the anger in her eyes. She turned on her heel and walked briskly down the hill.

Billy Tork, the gravedigger, picked up his

shovel and began throwing heaps of dirt mixed with crystalline jewels of ice into the grave while the wind wailed through the mountains.

Chapter 6

Charley knew he had cause to be angry with Bo, but the deputy apologized with such tearful sincerity that he had to forgive him.

Bo retired to his room, and Charley sat brooding. It was dark and snow was falling.

Dr. Hopkins had come in earlier with further depressing news, telling how several men of the town were preparing to venture out into the mountains in a greed-inspired search for the money. It was a foolhardy plan that only money-hungry men could conceive. The odds of finding the money were almost nil, but the lust for easy wealth overrode rational considerations.

The worst part was that right now the town needed all its men. No one knew the exact size of the Murphy gang, but rumor had it that Noah Murphy at times led two dozen men. They were reported to be trained gunmen, ruthless killers who could pack as much wallop as a band twice their size. Dry

Creek might soon face a siege, and several of its most hardy men were about to take off on a fool's mission for money that wasn't theirs. But Charley knew it would do no good to try to convince them to stay behind. He would let them go, and those left would make a defense as best they could, if it came to that.

Dr. Hopkins had told Charley that many of the townspeople apparently didn't believe Rand's claim that Charley knew where the money was. But neither were they convinced Charley had planned to tell them about the threat of the Murphy gang. Many harsh words were being spoken against the marshal because of that.

Charley knew that Rand's words had not risen from any deep concern for the community. Apparently the gambler's dislike for Charley went beyond anything the marshal had guessed. It mystified Charley somewhat, for he was not himself a vengeful person and could not fully understand those who were. Whatever his motivation, Rand had surely managed to get Charley into a fine mess.

The door opened and Sarah rushed in. Charley could tell she had been crying.

"Charley, I can't stand it, not another moment! I've tried to get along with her, but she won't let me. Please, Charley, you've got to get me away from her—"

"Sarah, hold on—what are you talking about?"

"I'm talking about Kathy, Charley. The things she has been saying about you—I can't stand it!"

Charley frowned. Kathy? Talking against him? That didn't sound believable. Kathy had always been a friend.

"Sit down, Sarah . . . here. Now just settle down and tell me what the problem is."

Sarah looked at Charley. She could see the hurt in him, and knew that the strain of facing a possible crisis directly after the death of his mother was exacting a hard toll. Suddenly she felt ashamed that she had come with news that would only make things harder for him. But the way Kathy had been talking, running him down—it was too much for Sarah to take, even though it made her feel petty now to talk about it.

"Charley, Kathy has been cold toward me. I didn't expect otherwise—we've never been friends, and I know she didn't like the idea of me living with her. I can stand unfriendliness, but I can't stand it when she talks against you. She says that Rand Cantrell was probably right about you and that money.

She said that you probably killed Willy Murphy yourself after he told you where it was."

Charley was aghast. "Why would she say that? Kathy knows I would never—"

"I don't know what she knows, Charley, just what she says. And I'll sleep in the street before I'll stay in the same house with her for another second. I'm sorry. Don't think me ungrateful for being allowed to stay there, but it's just getting to be too much."

"I understand. But where will you stay if you don't stay there?"

"With the Widow Thompkins. We're friends, and she won't care. I think she would like to have the company." Sarah paused and looked sadly at the marshal. "Charley, why are people saying such things? How can they turn on you so?"

"I don't know. Maybe Rand is mad because I trounced him a while back. The other folks . . . well, they're just ready to talk, to do anything to give a little excitement to their lives, I suppose. Dr. Hopkins says many of them don't really believe all Rand's tales. What scares me is that folks seem more interested in trying to find that money than preparing for the fight that's coming."

"Do you really think the Murphy gang will come back?" Sarah asked.

"Maybe, and I'm dreading it bad. They're killers of the worst sort, Sarah. I've heard of no other gang the size of them, and none more cruel."

"Charley, you're scaring me."

"You ought to be scared. Everyone should be. There was another mountain town they burned a couple of years ago—I was through there about a month after it happened, and folks were still dazed from it all. Almost a quarter of the population was killed and a lot of property destroyed.

"Murphy's men are a little army, all of them vicious. They enjoy killing and burning. Of all the gangs I've heard of, they're the worst, in my book. I just wish ol' Willy Murphy had died before he ever got to your place."

They heard a horseman ride quickly up on the street outside the office, riding up fast and hard. Charley tensed. The rider stopped just outside. For a moment there was silence.

"Listen to me, Dry Creek!" The shout came from the horseman. Charley moved to the window. The man was sitting astride a big stallion in the middle of the street.

"Listen to me! This town has money that belongs to us! You got two days to turn it over or you'll see what it's like when Noah

Murphy burns a town! That's the word from Noah Murphy!"

Bo emerged from the back room, strapping his gunbelt around his waist. Charley directed Sarah to the side of the room, where she crouched behind the desk, and Bo and Charley went to the door. Charley reached cautiously for the latch, then threw it open. He lunged out onto the sheltered porch, Bo right after him. The horseman turned, faced him, and began to grin.

"Marshal, have you come to turn yourself over to us?"

Charley shook his head. His hand slipped to the butt of his gun. "No sir. I'm not going anywhere. And I don't think you are either."

The horseman leaned forward now, frowning. "What did you say?"

Charley unleathered his gun. Leveling it on the rider, he spoke with deliberate coolness. "You heard me. Down off that horse. If you move your hand toward your gun, I'll blow you away. You understand?"

The rider was incredulous. "If I don't come back, Noah will come in here shooting no matter what happens."

Charley clicked back the hammer of his .44. The rider gaped, then apparently realized that the marshal was serious. He began

65

to dismount. As soon as his boots hit the snow he raised his hands. His horse moved away from him, leaving him standing alone, looking rather pitiful and helpless, a sharp contrast to the cocky figure he had cut moments before.

"Slip that gun out of your belt and drop it, then step forward two steps," Charley instructed. As the outlaw obeyed, Charley side-spoke to Bo.

"We got a new situation now. That's Farril Royster, one of Noah's old-time gang members. As long as we've got him we got an ace up our sleeve in dealing with Noah. The old boy made a blunder when he sent him in. I guess he figured we would be too surprised to try to take him."

A gun blast tore open the night. Farril Royster jerked, gasped, and pitched forward. Blood stained the back of his leather jacket, spreading out slowly to run into the snow. Charley stared in shock and Bo cursed.

Charley rushed into the street past the prone outlaw. He knew Royster was dead without checking, for the shot had struck him in the center of his body, no doubt tearing up his vitals. Charley wanted whoever fired that shot. Whoever it was had knocked out Dry Creek's only chance of gaining an advantage over the Murphy gang.

Charley had seen no flash of fire to give away the location of the gunman, and a quick check with Bo revealed he had noticed nothing either. Charley looked into windows and checked alleys, but it proved futile. So with a low curse he turned away and moved back to where the outlaw lay dead in the snow. He nudged the body with his foot. His first instinct had spoken truly. Farril Royster was dead.

"Well, Bo, we've had it for sure now," Charley said. "Having Royster for a hostage was the best chance we had to settle this without a fight."

"Who shot him, Charley?"

"I got no idea. Could have been Rand doing it to make things worse, could have been somebody scared and wanting to eliminate one of Murphy's gunmen."

People began to emerge from the buildings lining the street. They drew silently toward the dead outlaw and the somber marshal and deputy who stood looking down at him. They gathered in a circle around them, no one speaking, everyone scared and wondering what would come next. All had heard the warning carried by the outlaw.

Kathy stood at the rear of the crowd, Rand Cantrell a few feet from her. She eyed Charley with a cutting, harsh gaze, then glanced at Rand, who wore a smug smile.

Sarah emerged from the office and made her way to Charley's side. The marshal slipped his arm around her and drew her close, not concerned with the glances that passed between many of the onlookers. At that moment Charley couldn't care less about the opinions of the people. He had sworn to protect them and had done his best to fulfill that promise, but so far they had done only the very things that would harm them most. If it wasn't for folks like Dr. Hopkins and Sarah, this town would hardly be worth defending, or so it seemed to Charley.

Kathy watched him holding Sarah close to him, and her expression grew cold and haughty. When Rand headed toward the saloon she went after him, calling his name softly. He turned, then tipped his hat with his finger and smiled to see the lady approaching.

"Evening, ma'am. What can I do for you?"

"That isn't the question, Mr. Cantrell. I think once you hear what I have to say you'll agree that it's me who's done something for you."

Rand's quick smile flashed again. "That's an intriguing statement, ma'am. Step inside with me and we'll discuss it further."

Kathy balked. The Lodgepole was a man's place where women of decent raising didn't go. She said as much to Rand, and he smoothly apologized for what he termed his "indiscretion."

"I'm living in Mabel Hanna's old house," Kathy said. "Wait until everyone has gone to bed, and slip over a bit past midnight. I have something to discuss with you that you'll find very interesting, if I read you right. You might say we have a common goal, in a way."

"I'll be there, ma'am."

"I'll be waiting."

Kathy turned and moved quickly down the street. Rand watched her retreating form. An intriguing and mysterious lady, this Kathy Denning. He entered the Lodge-pole.

Word began spreading throughout the town of Dry Creek—the suspected attack from the Murphy gang was more than a suspicion. The little mountain town had two days to prepare itself for a siege.

Chapter 7

After Charley saw to the disposal of Farril Royster he began scouring the town, searching for some clue to who might have fired the shot and also trying to put together some plan for defense.

The town wasn't well-suited for such, for it was bordered by high, rugged hills that would afford plenty of protection for any sniper who might conceal himself there. Charley hoped that Noah wouldn't take that approach, for the people of Dry Creek would be pinned inside their dwellings.

Charley studied the dark street. As soon as he had begun his walk about the town, faces in the windows had vanished, kerosene lamps had winked out, and the street had become as silent as a grave.

He inspected the southern side of the wide street. On one end were several residences scattered in an uneven row, with the hardware store close beside them. Then the cafe, the gun shop, a handful of shops, the Lodgepole Saloon, and a few deserted old buildings, including the old livery. The facing side held another saloon, the Mansfield. Adjoining it was the Ketchum Boarding House, along with a laundry, the general merchandise store, a feed store, and Gertie Sander's seamstress shop. The church house sat off the main street several yards, on a slight hill. Adjacent to it was the knoll dotted with tombstones. It seemed a bit out of balance to Charley to realize that in the same ground where his mother lay newly buried, the worthless Willy Murphy also was interred, and Farril Royster soon would be.

Charley paused in the center of the street, looking around him. If the Murphy gang attacked from the cover of the hills, there would be little to do but wait them out and hope for an occasional shot at them. Somehow Charley suspected they wouldn't fight so covertly. Most likely they would ride into the main street, burning and shooting, doing their best to kill and terrorize. From what he knew of the Murphy gang, that seemed more their style.

If they did attack so openly, Charley wanted to have the town's men in the safest fighting position possible, some place where they could have a good range of fire into the streets without being overly exposed.

But that was assuming the townsfolk would go along with Charley in fighting the

Murphy gang at all. Right now the marshal wasn't sure just where he stood in the eyes of the people.

Apparently quite a few actually suspected Charley of being in league with the Murphys in some way, or at least of killing Willy Murphy after digging out of him the whereabouts of the money. Those people probably assumed Charley had the cash hidden somewhere. Even some who still believed in his honesty seemed to think he had been negligent about warning the town of the danger it was in.

Charley put his hand on his pistol grip and looked around him.

There was a row of second-story windows above the Mansfield Saloon and the boarding house. From those a man could have a good sweep of most of the street below while still being hidden behind thick walls himself. From that vantage point a group might make an able defense.

Charley huddled in the thickness of his leather coat and moved back toward the jailhouse. He procured a tobacco bag from his pocket and slipped off his gloves long enough to roll a cigarette. Striking the match on the porch column, he lit the tobacco and thought over his situation.

He could see why some folks who didn't know him well might suspect him of having taken that Murphy money, or at least of knowing where it was. After all, many of those folks were greedy themselves and even now were spending the night in the cold forest rather than their homes because they wanted so badly to find that stolen cash.

Charley saw the irony in trying to protect the same people who were whispering about him behind his back. But he wouldn't let that affect the way he did his job. He would stand up to the Murphy gang alone if it became necessary.

Charley would be willing to stand up to the devil himself if it was Sarah he was protecting. Surprising, the way he was beginning to feel about her. In the past she had been just another female to him, but now . . .

Funny that such a thing should happen at such a difficult time as this. Just when he suspected that he was falling in love he was being forced to put his life on the line. And if Rand's crusade against him kept going, there might not be more than a handful of folks willing to fight alongside him.

He looked over at the Lodgepole Saloon, still lit up and running despite the late hour.

It closed its doors only on Sundays, and then merely because the town law required it.

Charley strode across the street toward the log building. He figured Rand would be there at his usual place at the gambling table, or perhaps leaned up against the bar. He wanted to have a talk with the gambler.

When he entered he immediately felt the icy stares that greeted him. He knew then that Rand hadn't limited his talking to the funeral.

He saw Rand at the bar with a shot of amber whiskey in his hand. He was talking to some of the local men, who looked very interested and concerned about what he was saying. Charley could guess what he was talking about.

Rand noticed Charley approaching across the room, and for a brief second there flashed across his handsome face a smile that Charley found irritating. He had the sensation of being a teased child, or a puppet manipulated by the gambler.

"Hello, Marshal. Funny you should come in—we were just talking about you."

"And you had plenty to say, I'll bet."

The gambler sipped his drink, dark eyes sparkling above the glass. "What's wrong, Charley? You sound defensive."

"What's wrong is that this town is going to be under siege before long and all of you are sitting here drinking and running your mouths instead of doing anything about it. We've got to stop Noah Murphy from burning this town, and believe me, he's capable of doing it."

"Know a lot about Noah Murphy, do you?"

Charley's temper flared at the cool, pregnant comment. But he swallowed down his anger and managed to keep calm.

"I know a little. What are you getting at, Rand?"

The gambler glanced around him. Deliberately adopting the countenance of a man performing a painful duty, he looked down at the amber liquid in his shot glass and spoke in a low, smooth voice.

"Well, Charley, I'm getting at the same thing I talked about at your mother's burial. It seems you have sparked a lot of interest in our town on the part of Noah Murphy."

"He's interested because he thinks I've got his money or know where it is."

"Do you?"

"I answered that question already. I got no idea where it is. Willy Murphy died without telling."

"Don't take offense, Marshal, but how do we know that's true?"

Charley was having trouble controlling his temper now. He wasn't sure how much longer he could restrain himself in the presence of the arrogant, rumor-spreading gambler.

"If I knew where that money was, and if I was as dishonest a fellow as you seem to think, then I wouldn't be hanging around here, would I? I'd be long gone by now."

The gambler never lost his calm. Casually he took another sip, rolling the remnant of the liquor around in his glass and watching the swirling patterns it made. Then he looked up at Charley.

"I've been thinking on that very point," Rand said. "And I think I understand why it is you're still around. I'll confess I can't prove that you know where that money is, but look at the facts. First you come riding in with the body of Willy Murphy, saying his brother shot him. Maybe he did, maybe not. Just after you come in, you have a good chance to warn the town about this danger we're in—you know as well as me how many people were gathered there staring at those bodies—but still you say nothing. Your deputy overhears you talking to the doctor and

Sarah Redding about hidden money. Then the next day at the funeral of your mother you tell the town about the threat of Noah Murphy only after I first bring up what Bo Myers told me. It makes a sensible man suspect that if I hadn't spoken up you would have said nothing about it at all.

"Now there seems to me to be a logical explanation about just why you wouldn't be out in the mountains getting that money right now. Maybe you were telling the truth when you said Noah Murphy shot his brother, and we know that he is still roaming the mountains. We know that he would like to get his hands on you. Maybe the reason you're still here is simply that you're afraid to go out and claim that money while Noah's in the area. Maybe you want him to come raiding this town in the hope that he'll get himself killed and you can be free to take that cash. That's what I've been discussing with the men here, and let me tell you, there are many besides me who suspect the same."

Charley knew from the looks he was receiving that, in his last statement at least, Rand spoke the truth. The gambler was a convincing man, and his lies had taken root in suspicious minds. The frustrating thing was, there was nothing Charley could say to vindicate himself.

"Rand, you're a liar and a scoundrel, and any man who listens to you is a fool. I won't stand here and argue anymore. No matter what you think about me, the fact remains that everyone in this town potentially is facing death if we don't band together to hold out against Noah Murphy. I'd thrash you right now, like I did a while back, but I'll admit I need your gun and your support too much for that this time. We'll take care of our problems after all this is over. Are you going to stand with me or not?"

Rand drained the last of his drink. "I don't see that we're dependent on you for our defense, Marshal. And we haven't been sitting by and waiting for Noah Murphy to come, either. We have our own plans, sir, and quite frankly we don't feel you are trustworthy enough to be in charge. So it looks like I, and not you, will be coordinating this defense, should Noah Murphy truly be rash enough to attack the town." He smiled at Charley, who stood clenching his fists and imagining how good it would feel to smash the smug gambler's nose.

"Stick with me, Rand. It will be better if we're all fighting together," Charley said.

78

"Sorry, Marshal. The decision is made. Now if you don't mind, I'll take my leave. I've got a card game over there waiting—"

A loud, high-pitched scream echoed down the street. Charley turned.

"Sarah . . ."

He bolted for the door. The scream came again. Others in the saloon followed him.

He paused on the boardwalk and looked around, drawing his pistol. He heard the muffled sound of Sarah's voice, and his eyes were drawn to a movement in the alleyway toward the end of the opposite side of the street. He pounded across the snow toward the commotion.

Sarah was struggling in the arms of men Charley at first couldn't recognize. Then a face turned toward him, and he stopped, shocked.

William Branton and Max Franklin, two of the town's better-known merchants, stared at him with guilt and a hefty dose of fear. Franklin had a scratch down the left side of his face from Sarah's fingernails.

"Let her go!"

Franklin glanced at Branton, apparently reluctant to obey Charley's order. Charley raised his pistol and deliberately clicked back the hammer.

"I'll blow the heads off both of you, if you don't let her go *now*."

Branton went pale, and Franklin looked like a cornered rabbit. The pair took their hands off Sarah as if she suddenly had become red-hot, and the disheveled, weeping young woman ran straight for Charley, wrapping her arms around his waist. Charley continued glaring at the two men, not lowering the pistol.

Branton managed to choke out, "Charley —put that down. We let her go like you said."

Charley addressed Sarah without taking his eyes off the men. "What were they up to, Sarah?"

"They wanted me to take them to where the money was," she said. "They said they'd beat me if I didn't."

"Branton . . . Franklin—is that true?"

Franklin grinned weakly, putting forth his hands. "We didn't mean any harm—we were just funning her a little—"

The muzzle of Charley's pistol dropped slightly. The night was split by the roar of the shot and the responding scream of Franklin. Then the pistol roared again, two more times.

When the gunsmoke faded, the stunned

crowd that had gathered behind Charley saw the two men standing with their faces hidden in their arms, their bodies quaking. Only after a full ten seconds did Franklin dare look around him again, and Branton waited even longer.

The bullets had entered the ground inches from the feet of the two men, kicking up the dirt around their boots. Charley once more clicked back the hammer of his pistol.

"The next ones are in your guts unless you're out of my sight in five seconds. *Move!*"

The men took off at a dead run, Branton whimpering audibly as he pushed his way through the stunned crowd. Into the alley beside the Lodgepole they ran, disappearing into the darkness, running back to wives who would scold them for not finding out where the money was.

Only after they were gone did Charley holster his gun. He looked sternly around at the crowd. "If any one of you ever lays hands on Sarah again—or Dr. Hopkins, or me, for that matter—that man will find himself very dead. That's a promise."

He put his burly arm around the trembling woman at his side and walked briskly to the jailhouse.

Rand came to the front of the crowd and gestured toward the jailhouse after Charley and Sarah entered.

"See that, folks? He's willing to threaten the lives of all of us just to protect his little group of friends. He doesn't care about the welfare of you, me, or anyone else—just so his own are protected and the secret of that hidden money doesn't get out. Is that the man you want protecting this town against Noah Murphy? Is it?"

The crowd mumbled, murmured voices of dissent rising. Rand waved down the speakers, then looked across the group dramatically.

"Back there in the saloon a few minutes ago some of the men did me the honor of asking me to lead this town's defense against the Murphy gang. I'm willing to do that if you will give me the word that you're behind me. Do I have your support?"

There rose a loud cry of affirmation. Rand bowed and nodded like a successful politician on election day, and the crowd gathered around him, hustling him back toward the Lodgepole Saloon. From his office overlooking the street Dr. Hopkins watched the procession. He looked weary and sad. Letting the curtain drop from his wrinkled fingers he moved back into the musty office.

The revelry continued for some time, but at midnight Rand slipped out the door and headed on down the street toward the Mabel Hanna house, where Kathy Denning awaited him.

Chapter 8

When the sun rose over the snowy peaks the following morning, it cast its glow onto a band of sleeping citizens of Dry Creek who lay shivering and cold beside a scarcely flickering fire, their only shelter a crude tent and their only protection from the cold their thick clothing and heavy woolen blankets. They had rushed into the snowy wilderness too quickly to make better provision for themselves.

This little band, led by Abel Filson and Martin Arlo, had been forced to move quickly, for others had gone into the forests ahead of them in search of the Murphy money. No one had a clue about where to search, but none was willing to put aside the absurd hunt, for it was just remotely, deli-

ciously possible that by sheer chance someone might stumble upon it.

Filson and Arlo had led their little group
of treasure-seekers to the area of Sarah Redding's farm, for that had been where Willy
Murphy had died. Whether Willy had hidden the money, as Charley Hanna had said,
or whether Charley had hidden it himself,
as a lot of townspeople were saying, it
seemed likely to be somewhere close by.

Or so reasoned these money-hungry men
of Dry Creek who two days ago would have
scoffed at the idea they would ever pursue
stolen money with the full intention of keeping it. But two days ago such a prospect
would have been laughable, a fantasy with
no connection to their mundane, weary
world.

Now that the prospect was real, things
looked suddenly different to the usually
moral folks, and a kind of fever gripped
them. Now the same Abel Filson and Martin
Arlo who sat on the deacon's pew on Sunday
mornings in Dry Creek's only church were
willing to divide among themselves money
that had been taken from a Denver bank.

Arlo shook himself awake as the sun
burned down on his face, and it took him a
moment to piece together his situation and

recall just why he was lying on cold earth rather than his warm featherbed back in town. Sitting up, he rubbed his head and yawned, the cold morning air slicing painfully into his lungs. Every joint in his body ached from the stiffening effect of the cold and the iron hardness of the ground.

Filson stirred awake beside him and rose up, bleary-eyed and confused. Seeing Arlo, he grunted a sullen greeting and shook his head like a dog flinging water off its ears.

"Lord, that's hard ground," he muttered. The others were waking up now, also grumbling and cold. All told, there were five in the party. They had come together under the agreement that the money would be split evenly between them if any one of them found it. But in his heart each man in the group was completely ready to keep the full amount for himself if he was the one lucky enough to run across it, and if he could get away with it.

Filson rubbed a face covered with scruffy beard, and yawned. The men rose slowly, each gathering his blankets, one tossing a few branches onto the dying fire. The icy fragments of snow on the branches sizzled as they touched the red coals buried beneath the fluffy heap of ash at the base of the fire.

"Where we going to look?" asked Filson after the fire was built up again.

Arlo was filling a tin coffeepot with snow in preparation for making coffee. He shrugged. "Maybe we should go to Sarah Redding's house and start there."

One of the men sat on a fallen log, pulling on his boots. "Do you think Charley Hanna really knows where that money is?" he asked.

Arlo said, "No. I don't think he knows, I really don't. If he did he would be gone. He'd be off living it up in Denver or someplace. I figure it happened pretty much like he told it. But that means the money is out here somewhere, just waiting for somebody to find it."

Filson was more skeptical. "I don't know, Martin. Maybe Charley knows more than he lets on."

One of the others pulled out an iron skillet and set it on the rocks to the side of the fire, then poked some burning wood beneath it with a stick. "Do you think Noah Murphy will try to get Charley or the other two?"

"No, and I don't think he'd come in against a whole town, neither."

The men fried several hunks of greasy bacon and thawed out a few thick slices of bread above the flames. The aroma caught in the crisp morning breeze and wafted tantalizingly through the forest. When the coffee began to boil, tin plates and pewter forks and spoons were distributed and the group sat down to a simple but satisfying breakfast.

Immediately afterward they began their search. It was at first a disorganized affair, until Arlo again voiced his belief that the search could most logically be made beginning at Sarah Redding's house. The others agreed, some almost reluctantly, for so gripped were they with the fever for easy money that they hated to take the time for a systematic search.

The men rode toward the Redding house rather nervously, looking around them as they traveled. They sought not only for some possible sign that might lead them to the money—a hidden footprint, an incompletely obscured trail—but also for others from Dry Creek who were in the mountains making their own search. And for Noah Murphy, who was a threat they were unwilling to openly acknowledge, but which hung in the back of their minds like a stubborn bad memory.

The trail on which they rode was snow-dusted, leading beneath spruces that reached down with evergreen branches to swipe at their heads, and pale-barked aspens laden with frost. Through the timber they saw the sky, fairly clear this morning but still holding dark and threatening clouds on the far horizon, and silver-white mountains that loomed majestic and rocky above the timberline skirting the barren peaks.

But none in the group took time to view the scenery, for all eyes were on the earth and the trail. When Arlo halted within a few hundred yards of the Redding house, the others stopped behind him. Arlo bent over and studied the snow on the ground beside the horse's hooves.

"What it is, Martin?"

"Tracks—a bunch of 'em. Leading toward the Redding house."

"Yeah—I see. I wonder who?"

"Some of the others, I'll betcha," growled a man in the rear. "Beat us to it, looks like."

"Probably. But let's approach slow and careful and be ready to retreat if it comes to that."

The men started forward again, Arlo no longer looking at the trail but instead scanning the dark woodland around him. He ducked a drooping aspen branch and goaded his horse over a rocky crest in the trail. They entered a region where the pathway circled amid an outcropping conglomeration of boulders backed by snow-lined scrub brush and a few occasional cedars.

Winding through the rocks, Arlo came out onto the road that led toward the Redding house. He rode as far as he could without exposing himself to view from the house, then stopped. Filson pulled up beside him and the others paused behind.

"What are you thinking, Martin?"

"I don't know . . . those tracks appeared fairly fresh, just a little new snow in them. Probably some of the others looking for the money, but then . . ."

"What are we waiting on?" said a grumbler at the rear. "Let's ride on and see if there's sign around that house."

"Be patient, Fred. We got to be careful about this."

"Careful, you say? While we sit here being careful some of the others are picking up sign of that money. I say let's get on."

The speaker was Fred Gearhart, a stocky, square-jawed man with thinning hair and a sour disposition. He had joined the searching party reluctantly, preferring to look on his own, but had been convinced to band with the others when someone pointed out Noah

Murphy's possible presence in the mountains. But even then Gearhart seemed uncertain of his commitment to the group and appeared ready to take off on his own at the slightest provocation. His disgruntled spirit had spread to some of the others in the party as well.

"Hang it, Fred, we will get on. But do you want to ride up on that house if Noah Murphy and his boys have been around here recently? Maybe that's where they are— Sarah being in town and all, there ain't nobody there to keep them out."

Gearhart's forehead crinkled into a meaty, hand-sized expanse of wrinkles, and his jowls drooped like those of a boxer dog. His heavy brown eyebrows tilted upward in the center, and he looked the image of exasperation.

"If Noah Murphy's around here, then we've had it for sure," he said. "I'll grant you that. But how we supposed to find out? If you want to sit here and worry about Noah Murphy, then you can. But I'm riding in. Anybody with me?"

A thin man in a brown water-spotted hat twisted his mouth beneath a jungle of drooping mustache and said, "I'll go, Fred. We won't find no money sitting here."

A third man, toward the rear, seemed bolstered by the decision of the other and quickly expressed his agreement. But Arlo felt a growing sense of uneasiness that was peculiarly intense. He suddenly wished he had never come here. He turned an appealing eye to Filson, who looked almost ashamed as he said, "I'll go with them, Martin. There probably ain't nobody at that house no way."

Gearhart dug his heels into his chestnut mare's flanks and pulled out into the lead. Rounding the concealing bend, he rode bravely toward the house. The others followed, Filson going last.

Arlo hesitated, pursing his lip. He had been outvoted, but something still told him not to round the bend after the others. They rode around, leaving him alone.

A high-powered rifle barked in the morning stillness, followed by a horrible cry, then more shots. Arlo's hand tensed around the saddle horn, and he listened to a sudden tumult of whinnying, rearing horses, yelling men, and roaring guns.

He heard a rider coming back from the clearing, then another. Filson rounded the bend at a dead run, screaming at Arlo to follow. There was terror in his voice. Only

91

one other followed him—the fleshy, gasping Gearhart.

Arlo goaded his horse after the others, running as if a demon were in fast pursuit. He guessed that if Noah Murphy and his boys were what inspired this run, a demon might be a preferable pursuer.

Filson and Gearhart were sticking to the main road, heading toward Dry Creek. Arlo almost followed them, but the sound of more riders behind him spurred a sudden change of mind and he cut into the dark woodland trail from which he had emerged minutes before, ignoring the slapping, cutting branches that whipped about his face.

A short distance off the road he entered the rock area and pulled his horse to a stop. Dismounting with clumsy haste, he grasped the reins and led the animal around behind the largest of the rocks. His mouth was dry, his lips forming a silent prayer of desperation. Riders dashed past on the road.

Then there was a silence as sudden as the outbreak of shots moments before. Arlo heard the loud beating of his heart. His horse gave a low whinny and he tried to quieten it.

Then he heard horses coming back up the

road on the other side of the trees. This time they were not running.

"That's far enough," said a gruff voice. "Get down."

"Please . . . what are you going to—"

"Shut up, fat man. Get down. You too, friend."

Arlo closed his eyes. He felt ill. Whoever it was had Gearhart and Filson. It had to be the Murphy gang.

"What are you gents doing out here?"

"We came . . . we came looking for . . ."

Arlo recognized Gearhart's voice, and from the words and tone it was clear that he was grasping for some explanation—any explanation—other than the true one.

"Spit it out, fat man. What are you doing out here? And why did you ride up on the house like you did?"

"We . . . we know the person who lives there, and we came to visit—"

Sudden, interrupting laughter. Arlo hugged the white rocks and bit his lip, trembling from more than the cold.

"You're a liar. Turn around."

"What?"

"Turn around. You ain't going to want to see this."

"Oh no. No."

"Suit yourself."

Arlo bit his lip with each jolting roar of the pistol as it cleared its throat. Someone laughed when it was done.

"What do you reckon they were doing, Noah?" someone on the road asked.

"I don't know. It don't matter. That's just four less to worry about when it comes time to ride into town. I don't figure that marshal plans to cooperate, and I'm inclined to burn the town even if he does. Go through the pockets of these and see if they got anything worth keeping. I'll get the ones in the clearing."

Arlo slid down to his rump on the earth behind the white rocks that had saved him from detection. Try as he would, he couldn't stop trembling. His horse shuffled quietly in the snow, looking down at its master as if confused by his strange posture.

Chapter 9

When Martin Arlo rode into Dry Creek alone, he drew many stares and heard many whispers. Everyone knew he had been among those who rode into the mountains in search of the hidden money, and now that he was returning—alone—curiosity was aroused. And when he rode without stopping straight to the marshal's office, there was murmuring among the people.

Arlo found Charley finishing his morning coffee. He was too distraught to notice the lines of worry and tension that lined the marshal's eyes.

"Hello, Martin. What brings you back?"

"It was a massacre, Charley . . . a massacre." He spit the words out in a tense whisper. Charley felt a cold shiver run through him.

"Who, Martin?"

Arlo sank into a chair beside the oaken table that sat against the side wall. "All of them, Charley, all of them. I'm the only one who got away."

"Exactly who are you talking about?"

The shaken man said, "Filson and Gearhart and Paul and Zeke Stone. Noah Murphy and his boys did it. Filson and Gearhart were murdered in cold blood, shot right in the head after they were caught."

Somehow the news did not shock Charley greatly; the way things had been going, he half expected such.

"You sure it was Murphy?"

"Yes. I heard them talking after they

95

killed them. I was in the rocks just off the road that leads to Sarah Redding's house. It was there that they killed them."

Charley strode over to the window and pulled back the curtain. He stared across the street. "This means Murphy wasn't bluffing. We've got until tomorrow night. I just hope they really hold off that long."

"Charley, you got my support in anything we can do to defend ourselves. I was a fool to go off into the woods like that—all of us were. I'll fight hard as I got to, to make up for that mistake."

Charley looked with appreciation at Arlo. Even as simple a word of support as he had just given seemed a tremendous boost just now.

"Thanks, Martin. We'll be needing the help of every man."

"Do you have a plan?"

"The town is divided. Rand Cantrell has been spreading his stories about me, making it look like me and Sarah and Dr. Hopkins are all in league together to get that Murphy money. The fact is none of us know where the money is, but the more I say that the more folks don't believe me.

"They've even started trying to beat the information out of us. Last night Branton and Franklin tried to force it out of Sarah. I got her at the Widow Thompkins' place right now, with Bo guarding the door. And folks are refusing to cooperate with me in planning a defense. They're turning to Rand as their leader, and he's playing it for all it's worth.

"I can't figure why he's so set to stir up trouble. I know the man don't like me, but it's gone beyond that now. I think he just likes the attention, having folks follow after him and all."

Arlo shook his head. "This is no time for that. This town needs to be unified to stand up to the Murphy boys. They're cold-blooded. I know that firsthand now."

"So will this whole town pretty soon, Martin. I just wonder if Rand will prove as capable of leading the people as he thinks he is."

Arlo stood up, fingering his hat. "Maybe when folks hear what happened out there they'll realize how serious this is."

Charley shrugged. "Maybe. Martin, I'm deputizing you here and now. You go out and spread the word that I'll meet everybody in the churchyard at ten o'clock. Right now I got to go talk to some widows who don't know they're widows just yet."

The marshal pulled on his hat and stepped outside. Arlo watched him leave, then went to the cabinet where Charley kept his whiskey. Pouring himself a stout drink, he downed it. Glancing into the shaving mirror hanging above the pitcher and basin in the corner, he said, "C'mon, deputy. Do your work."

He pulled on his hat and walked out into the street.

The crowd began to converge on the church house well before ten. Rand was there, and much attention was focused on him. People who before had loathed the gambler as a parasite now spoke of him with great respect, and men and women who had been friends of Charley's for years talked contemptuously of the marshal.

"He ain't concerned about this town," a man declared to Preacher Bartlett. "He was after that money, and now that Rand Cantrell called his hand he's trying to save face. He didn't care that the Murphy boys will overrun this town."

The preacher made a feeble defense of the marshal, whom he had always respected before, but his words were faltering and uncertain. With the bad talk about Charley that was floating around, he was beginning to wonder if perhaps some of the accusations were true.

Charley climbed to the top of the church-house steps and raised his hands. Gradually the crowd quieted, and dozens of hostile gazes focused on the marshal.

"Thank you all for coming out today. I don't need to tell you what the problem is. We're facing an attack from the Murphy gang as early as tomorrow night, and it's important that we have a defense plan worked out."

"Whose fault is it that Murphy and his boys are coming, Charley?" Someone called out from the crowd. A responding hostile murmur whispered through the group.

Charley tried to locate the speaker amid the jumble of faces. "It ain't nobody's fault," he said. "The way I see it—"

"The way I see it, it's obvious whose fault it is!" said another voice.

Charley felt his temper rising. He did his best to squelch the growing rage within him. Losing his temper could only make things worse.

"Like I was saying," he continued, "we got to work up a defense against the Murphy gang before tomorrow night. If we don't, they'll ride in here and give us more trouble than you can imagine. If we all band together—"

Rand stepped forward. "Excuse me, Marshal," he said, "You're a little behind. We *are* banded together. We have been for some time now. And we are making a defense plan already. This meeting is a waste of time."

Charley glared coldly at the man. "We need to work together if this thing is going to work. And as your marshal, it seems to me that I should be the one to lead the defense.

"Most of you have probably heard by now that some of your neighbors were killed this morning by the Murphy gang while they were out looking for that money. And there are still other search groups out there that might be facing the same death this very minute. That's the kind of folks we're facing. I have experience with dealing with such, and it should be me that leads this town, not some loudmouthed gambler."

Rand smiled faintly as the crowd responded to Charley's comment with sounds of derision. Rand raised his hand to quiet them.

"Marshal," he said, "it seems to me that if you were so fired up about saving this town from the Murphy gang you would do the only manly thing possible—surrender your-self to them. Go to them, tell them what they want to know, fulfill their demands, and this town would be out of danger."

The crowd cheered the suggestion, and Charley's face reddened. After the noise died he responded.

"Things ain't that simple, Rand," he said. "For one thing, I can't tell them where the money is 'cause I don't know. And when they finally figured that out, they'd burn this town for spite. And now that Farril Royster is dead it's almost certain they'll attack no matter what. It's my duty to protect this town as best I can."

The crowd roared its disapproval, and Rand seemed to swell with pride to hear the evidence of the town's support of him. He had never before known the sweetness of being viewed with respect.

The gambler walked up the church steps and stood beside Charley. Smiling at the marshal, he turned and looked dramatically over the crowd. Charley started to speak, to order him down off the porch, but Rand again beat him to the punch.

"My friends, there is more to this than has yet been told. There is a further reason why Charley Hanna shouldn't be trusted to defend this town against the Murphy gang. He is, after all, their own kin."

That brought a sudden, overwhelming silence. Charley was every bit as shocked as the crowd.

"What are you talking about, Rand?" someone asked.

"Maybe Kathy Denning should be the one to explain this," Cantrell said. "Miss Denning, come up here, please."

Charley suddenly felt weak. Kathy stood on the edge of the crowd, her expression strangely hard and emotionless.

She walked up the steps. Charley looked imploringly at her, but she ignored him. She walked up and stood beside the gambler. The crowd was very quiet now, eager for an explanation of the puzzling pronouncement Rand had just made. For his part, Charley was so stunned he could say nothing.

"Just tell the folks what you told me last night," Rand said. "Speak up loud so everybody can hear."

Kathy's voice quaked slightly when she began speaking, but she talked loudly and with determination.

"Last night I talked to Mr. Cantrell, giving him information I thought was important," she said. "It wasn't an easy thing for me to do, but under the circumstances I had no choice.

"Charley Hanna has a far closer relationship with the Murphy gang than has been told so far. Mabel Hanna informed me that she was a sister of Lead Jack Murphy, the father of the Murphy brothers. Charley has been aware of that relationship all of his life. One of the things Mabel expressed concern about was Charley's interest in his cousins' activities. She wrote that he had talked many times about the money he knew they often had and how much he'd like to have some of it.

"And because of that I don't think it's wise to trust Charley to defend this town. I recommend that all of you give your support to Mr. Cantrell and, as soon as this situation is through, that Charley be removed from his office. Any man that has such a connection with a criminal gang should not serve as marshal of a town."

The crowd mumbled and shifted, staring at Charley. Rand looked haughtily at him. "Can you deny the truth of what was said, Marshal?"

"I deny every word. There's not a trace of truth in it. My mother had no connection to Lead Jack Murphy, and I've never made any of the statements Kathy just said I did. Rand, I don't understand why you spread lies like you do, and Kathy . . . of all the people in the world, why you? Why?"

Kathy turned a brutal gaze upon him, her lips set firmly. In her eyes was only the faintest hint of remorse. She turned and descended the stairs.

"Marshal, it looks like the decision has been made," said Rand. "This just isn't your town anymore."

"Not so fast, Cantrell," said Martin Arlo, who had been standing toward the front of the crowd throughout the meeting, looking increasingly angry.

He darted quickly up the stairs and pushed Cantrell aside. "Listen to me," he said. "I've known Charley Hanna for years, and in all of that time I've never seen him do one thing that would make me doubt his honesty. And if the lot of you were honest, you'd admit the same thing. He's a good man, and one who knows his business when it comes to doing his job. He had a good teacher—his pa.

"But Rand here is nothing but a two-bit, saloon-running gambler who likes to imagine he's a big man. He's had it in for Charley since Charley thrashed him that night a few months back. He's using you people to get back at Charley, that's all. I'm putting my money on Charley. I was foolish enough to take Murphy and his boys lightly once, but there won't be a twice. And I won't trust my safety to the direction of a jackass gambler!''

There arose a roar of dissent, but amid the voices Charley heard a few supportive cries, and the expressions on some of the faces indicated that a few were cheered to hear Arlo speaking up for the marshal.

After the hubbub died once more, Arlo spoke again, his voice lower. "I'm behind Charley Hanna. I believe there are those among you who agree. If you do, come on up here and stand with us. If this town is going to be split, we might as well make it a clear-cut division.''

For a moment there was no response, but then movement at the fringes of the crowd indicated some were accepting the challenge. One by one people began filing up to the church steps.

But when the last man stepped up onto the porch, it was obvious the majority of townspeople still supported Rand. A mere group of fifteen stood with Charley, not including Arlo and Sarah. Rand looked at the much larger crowd assembled with him and his confidence, which had been momentarily set back, swiftly returned.

"Well, you've had your say, Mr. Arlo," he said. "And now you've got your group. If you'll be on your way, the rest of us will begin planning further just how we're going to defend this town from the danger the marshal has brought upon it."

"Fine," snapped Charley. "You have your meeting. I got better things to do."

He left, followed by those who had declared their allegiance to him. They moved as a group down the street to the vicinity of the jailhouse, and Charley stepped onto the boardwalk to address them.

"I appreciate your support more than you can know," he said. "I was beginning to think that the whole blasted town has gone loco. We'll need to do some planning if our defense is going to hold out. I just hope Rand's group does as well as they think they will against Murphy and his boys. They don't know what they're facing. But right now there's something I got to do. You all meet me back here in an hour."

The little gathering dispersed, and Sarah approached Charley. "Charley . . . is it . . ."

"No, Sarah," he said, anticipating her question. "Those were lies that Kathy was spreading. I don't understand what's so turned her against me."

Sarah said nothing, but suspected she knew the answer. She was aware from the way Kathy had looked at Charley these past months that the lady was in love with him. But now the whole town was aware of the budding romance between Sarah and the marshal, and Kathy was understandably jealous. But to go so far as to spread lies about Charley . . .

"Sarah, I got to talk to Dr. Hopkins. I want you to go with me."

"Certainly, Charley."

Together they walked across the street and ascended the stairs to Dr. Hopkins' office. They found him inhaling steam from a kettle bubbling on the stove. It was obvious that his lungs had been giving him trouble today. Charley figured that's why the man had missed the town meeting.

"Howdy. Feeling bad?"

"The usual difficulty, Charley. Hello, Sarah. What brings you here? Rand causing his usual share of trouble?"

"More than his share. He's gone beyond what he said before. He's spreading new lies about me."

"What's he saying?"

"He said Ma was a sister to Lead Jack Murphy, that I'm a cousin to the Murphy boys and have tried to get in on their jobs in the past."

The old man dropped roughly in a chair. Charley quickly went to the doctor's side.

"Are you all right?"

"Yes. But I must tell you something—something that I encouraged Mabel to tell you herself before she died. Sit down, Charley, and listen to me.

"Rand was telling the truth when he said Mabel was a sister to Lead Jack. I know it's true, because I knew them both years ago."

Chapter 10

Charley stared blankly at the old doctor as if he didn't comprehend what he had said. Then his face twisted into a frown.

"Kathy was telling the truth?"

"About you being kin to the Murphy boys, yes. I'm sorry you had to find out like this, Charley.

"I knew your mother years ago, back in Kansas. That was before she ever met your pa, and I wasn't yet practicing medicine. I was a rough fellow, I'll confess, and I rubbed shoulders with a lot of the scum of this earth—including Lead Jack Murphy. The first time I saw him he was sitting at a cafe table with his sister—your mother, Charley.

"Your mother and I got to be good friends, and she confided in me about a lot of things, including how she worried about how her brother was getting into things he shouldn't. The first robbery Jack ever pulled was in St. Louis. His name got to be known and people started calling him Lead Jack because of how much ammunition he kept strapped in a belt around his waist. And as his reputation grew, the more ashamed Mabel got to be.

"She moved away not long after Lead Jack killed his first man," Dr. Hopkins continued, "and changed her name to Simmons. That's what she went by when she met your pa, and she never told him different. I didn't know what had become of her until I came to Dry Creek. When I saw her it brought back a lot of old memories, let me tell you! We talked, and I promised her I would never let her secret out. And until now I haven't.

"When this trouble with the Murphy boys came up, I told Mabel she ought to tell you about if. If a man is going to fight his own kin he has a right to know who they are. But Mabel died before she ever told you."

"Kathy said she found a written message. . . ."

The old man nodded. "That explains it. Mabel was probably writing that message to you, Charley. That was her way of telling you. But Kathy must have found it first."

Charley whistled. "Lord, what a thing to find out! Before, I would have busted the skull of any man who tried to link me up with the Murphy boys. I like to have busted Rand Cantrell's today."

Sarah interrupted hesitantly. "But Charley, Kathy still was lying when she said you had talked about getting involved with the gang. She talked like you knew all along you were kin to them and wanted to take advantage of it."

"She did. And I can't understand that. Kathy has always been a good family friend. Ma loved her like a daughter."

"Folks do strange things sometimes," Dr. Hopkins said. "You can't always predict them."

"Now I've got another problem," Charley said. "I told the whole town that I have no connection with the Murphys. Am I supposed to go right back out and deny it now?"

Dr. Hopkins shrugged. "I don't think it matters, Charley. Those who don't like you will believe what Rand says no matter what, and those who believe in you likely will stick with you to the end whether you tell them about this or not. But why say anything at all? Just let it go. I can't see that it will help for you to start shifting ground at the moment."

Charley pondered Dr. Hopkins' words. Twisting his lip, he nodded. "You're right. We might as well keep it our secret until this mess is finished. So as far as this town is concerned, I'm still denying any family connection with the Murphy gang. I'm still calling Rand a liar."

Charley and Sarah went back down into the street. Charley once again studied the windows on the second stories of the boarding house and the Mansfield Saloon.

"If we had gunmen up there they would have a wide sweep of the street," Charley pointed out to Sarah. "And if we had the street barricaded, maybe we could keep the Murphy gang from getting in close enough to set fires."

Charley's supporters returned and the meeting took place. The handful of men looked pitifully small. The marshal looked at the somber gathering on the jail porch and shook his head slowly.

"We ain't much of an army, are we? Let's hope Rand does a good job with his. We ain't got much chance of beating the Murphys unless he does."

Charley outlined his plan to the group. Using feed bags from the livery, furniture from the stores and houses, wagons, barrels, anything, the street would be barricaded on both ends. Men would be positioned at each barricade, and sharp-eyed riflemen would cover the street from the windows atop the boarding house and Mansfield Saloon. Every other alleyway would be barricaded also, as much as possible, so the town would be a makeshift fort.

But it would be a fort with two commanders. Charley feared that the double command would be what would undo the town, if anything would. But he couldn't give up his authority to Rand. The protection of Dry Creek was *his* job. He had sworn to protect the town and would do it if it killed him.

Charley answered questions that the men had about the defense, and as a group they walked out onto the main street and looked it over. The skies had cleared, but the cold was still biting and the street was still filled with snow, packed down now from the many feet that had walked across it.

Berkshire Novak, the town gunsmith, approached Charley. "I got an idea that might help us out," he said.

"What's that?"

"Gunpowder. I got some stored out back of the shop. It's in a vault, most of it. But it's dry—I always make sure of that. Get us some empty bottles, a few fuses . . ."

"And we got us some ready-made surprises for the Murphys," said Charley, smiling. "Good idea, Berk."

The marshal followed the lanky gunsmith to his shop, cutting through an alley toward the back of the building.

Novak stopped, looking perplexed. "It looks like somebody has been here."

Charley knelt and examined a multitude of relatively fresh tracks around a pitch-covered trapdoor. Novak reached for the leather strap that served as a handle and with a creak and groan the door opened to reveal a pitch-lined wooden chamber placed into the earth, large enough to hold several big kegs.

But there were no kegs in the chamber. It was empty. Novak looked incredulously into the hole, then turned to Charley.

"Who could have taken it? And why?"

Charley pursed his lips. "There's several that might have taken that powder. Let's hope it wasn't the Murphy gang. If they found that stuff we're in a bad way for certain. But it might not be them. I think we ought to have a talk with Rand about this."

Charley turned and strode off toward the Lodgepole. Novak followed. Charley pushed into the building, glaring around the room until he saw Rand seated at a corner table, some cronies around him.

"Well, hello, Marshal! Didn't expect to see you—"

"Shut up, Rand. What do you know about some gunpowder missing from Novak's shop?"

Rand frowned. "I don't know what you're talking about, Marshal. Are you trying to accuse me of—"

"That powder is needed for the defense of this town. If you know anything about it, start talking."

Rand looked at him coldly. "I haven't stolen any gunpowder, Marshal. Remember, I'm trying to defend this town too. I didn't even know there was gunpowder stored there."

Charley frowned, exasperated. He realized that even if Rand had taken the powder he would have no way of proving it. Certainly the gambler wasn't about to confess.

"Well, if you didn't take it, then Murphy's boys must have slipped in and dug it out. It wouldn't have been hard to do. If they were looking for powder it would be likely that they would look at a gunsmith's place first."

Cantrell pulled a long cigar from his pocket and lit it. He looked at Charley through the smoke and said, "I'd like to know what you have in mind for defending this town, Marshal, since you still insist on trying to do so even though almost everyone in the town wants me to do it. We might as well try not to interfere with each other."

"That's the first smart thing I've ever heard you say, Rand. It won't hurt to tell you. We're planning on barricading the streets and alleys and putting riflemen up in the windows of the Ketchum Boarding House and the Mansfield Saloon."

Rand nodded slowly. "Sounds logical. I'll have riflemen on top of the Lodgepole and some of the adjacent buildings."

"You have more riflemen than I do. Let's cooperate on this. Send some over to the other side of the street with my men."

"No. They all stay on this side."

Charley frowned. "But why? It would be a lot more effective if—"

"Sorry. I simply don't trust you. They'll all stay on this side of the street. And I'll keep an eye on you, too. Anybody who's fighting his own kin isn't to be trusted too far. For all I know, you might be siding with them."

Charley's throat tightened and his face grew red. Rand was pushing him, and it wouldn't take much more to push him too far.

"Rand, I'll do anything I have to, to keep this town safe."

"Anything?"

"You heard me."

"Then turn yourself over to the Murphy gang. You are what they want."

"We've gone over this before. I don't have their money, or know where it is. When whatever fool it was shot Farril Royster, this town's death warrant was signed. Murphy and his gang want revenge. Sending me out there would be nothing but throwing away a good gun when we need every one available."

Rand gave a short, derisive laugh. "So you say, Marshal. Very well, then, stay and fight.

But remember, it was because of you that Noah Murphy issued his ultimatum."

"Rand, you're a liar and a fool. You took on a lot of responsibility when you decided to be this town's guardian. I just hope you know what you're in for. When you bite off a hunk of the Murphy gang, it's a tough mouthful to chew."

A cry came from the street. Charley recognized the voice of Martin Arlo.

"Charley! Come quick!"

Charley turned and headed for the door, the saloon occupants following him. Rand looked vaguely disturbed, but he didn't let his thin, smug smile fade for more than an instant.

Charley stepped out onto the boardwalk, looking westward to the end of the street.

Horses came down the street. Draped across their saddles were stiff and pale dead men with blood soaking their shirts. They were the remainder of the men who had gone into the mountains to search for the Murphy money.

Chapter 11

The people on the street fell utterly silent, watching the parade of death.

Charley heard the hissing cry of a woman across the street, then saw her collapse to the boardwalk. Well she might; her brother was among the dead. The motion of her fall seemed to wrench the astonished crowd out of its stupor. Two of the more stalwart men who had emerged behind Charley from the saloon went out into the street and caught the lead horses by the reins, pulling them to a stop. The other horses stopped behind them.

Charley stepped out into the street. "Get 'em down," he ordered. "Quick as you can."

He looked around him. Almost all of the townsfolk were gathered on each side of the street, witnesses to the greatest horror Dry Creek had yet known. From the expressions on their faces Charley could tell that the true danger the town was facing was only now being fully realized by many of the townsfolk. Even Rand seemed taken aback, his face suddenly blanched.

Charley addressed the people. "Look at

it, folks . . . this is the way of the Murphy gang. This is the sort of thing typical of the men we'll be facing. They'll put your homes to the torch and murder your children and do things to your wives you don't want to think about. And instead of pulling together and preparing to stop them short of killing us all, this town has divided. The time has come to quit arguing and start getting ready for what's coming. 'Cause what's coming is going to be pure hell."

"And it's your kin bringing it!" a voice shouted from the crowd.

Charley turned a stern eye in the direction of the speaker. "I don't care if Noah Murphy is Preacher Bartlett's grandma—he's still an enemy. You want to know why he killed these men instead of taking them hostage? Because he wants a fight, that's why! He don't want to avoid it. He's ready to burn a town, and nothing is going to stop him. Unless it's us.

"Now there's a few of you who have stuck with me. The rest of you seem to think you should trust your safety to the orders of a no-'count gambler. I'm giving you a chance to change your minds. I've got a plan, but I need good men to carry it out. Do I have them?"

119

Charley could tell his words were having an effect. Men that before had been dead-set against him now glanced at each other with doubt in their eyes. Rand sensed he was losing his control. The gambler looked nervously at those around him, disturbed.

"It's not going to pay when things come down to the actual fight for everybody in town to be following a different drummer," Charley said. "If you are with me, come over here and stand beside me."

Men began to step down from the boardwalk, pushing past Rand to join Charley on the street. It was a handful at first, but then others followed, until when it was over there were more men at Charley's side than Rand's.

Charley smiled. The men Rand had remaining were those Charley had tangled with in the past, men with reason to hate him. But that was all right with Charley; at least now the sides were clear and he had a vastly increased team of fighters on his.

"Good. Real good," Charley said. "Now let's get those bodies out of here and talk about just what we're going to do."

Rand looked at Charley with a murderous expression, then wheeled about and entered the Lodgepole. His greatly reduced band of followers trailed in after him.

Kathy stood in front of the boarding house long after the other women who had been drawn out by the parade of dead riders vanished into the buildings. She watched Charley talking to the men in the street, his arms making sweeping gestures as he described his proposed street and alley barricades. The lady's eyes were brooding and thoughtful. Silently she stepped across the street, heading for the Lodgepole. She had never set foot inside the building before, but this time she felt she had no choice.

She found Rand seated at his usual corner table, frowning and brooding. His men were scattered around the saloon, away from him. Kathy walked directly up to him and sat down.

"Mr. Cantrell, I need to talk to you. I think we've made a mistake."

The gambler glanced harshly at her. "What do you mean?"

"I think it was wrong to lie about Charley Hanna and the Murphy gang."

"What lie? It's true that he's kin to Noah Murphy."

"Don't play games with me . . . you know what I mean. The lie was saying Charley

121

knew he was kin to them and that he's talked about getting in on their crimes. That was wrong. It should have never been said."

The gambler's stare stabbed into her. "You're changing your tune, my dear. Not more than a few hours ago you were ready to hang Charley Hanna. Why the change?"

Kathy looked away. "I don't know . . . it just wasn't right to lie."

Cantrell leaned forward, studying her. "Was it right for Charley to ignore you and take to Sarah Redding like he has?"

Kathy's face grew burning red. Rand seemed to have read motives and deep feelings she thought she had hidden.

He smiled. "It's more obvious than you think, Miss Denning. Love is a hard secret to keep."

Kathy lowered her eyes, feeling his gaze.

"Ah, I've embarrassed you. My apology. But don't feel ashamed. I think that you of all people should understand why Charley Hanna doesn't deserve to have all the trust being given to him by that bunch of fools who are ready to trust him with their lives."

"You didn't call them fools when they were following you."

Rand ignored the comment. "He jilted you, Miss Denning. Rejected you. Why are you defending him now? Do you think he deserves it?"

Kathy paused, thinking. "No."

"Then you'll keep our little secret?"

The pause was longer this time. At last Kathy nodded. "I won't say anything. I don't know how I could explain why I lied, anyway."

Rand smiled. "A good decision, Miss Denning. Here's to you." He raised his glass of whiskey and took a sip.

Outside in the street Charley was talking seriously to the men gathered around him.

"I have reason to believe the Murphy gang has their hands on a lot of gunpowder," he said. "A good number of barrels turned up missing from the gunsmithy this morning. We had plans to use that powder, but there's no way now. I'm afraid Murphy and his boys have the same idea. If they do, then we're liable to find ourselves scattered all over these mountains."

"What are we going to do with the women?"

"Children, old folks, and women we'll keep in the back of the boarding house. Just about everybody else will have a part to play."

The rest of the day passed with further

planning, and by evening the building of the barricades had begun. Lanterns and torches were brought out into the street to illuminate the work, and even the children were involved in dragging heavy furniture from the saloons and houses, the boarding house, and other places of business. Several of the huskier men went to the church house and began dragging the heavy pews out to form the basis of the barricade on that end of the street.

They filled the alleys with bags of feed from the livery until all the bags were used up. Then empty burlap sacks were found somewhere, and several of the town's youths went to work filling them with dirt and stacking them in the remaining unblocked alleyways. When even those were used up, the remaining alleys were blocked with all the extra furniture that could be found.

By the time the moon was shining clear in the cold night sky high above Dry Creek, the town was like a fortress. Each means of access to the central portion of the main street was blocked, and the townspeople were all within the boundaries of the makeshift fort, most of them crowded into the boarding house. There was much grumbling about being shifted to such uncomfortable quarters a full night before the expected attack was to occur, but Charley was taking no chances. He feared the Murphy gang might make their threat good early, so as to catch the town unprepared.

Rand gave only reluctant cooperation to Charley Hanna, keeping his handful of men in the Lodgepole, from where he would make his defense, he said. Charley didn't argue with him; the roof of the Lodgepole would make a good vantage point from which to fight. If Cantrell wanted to keep his men there, that was fine with Charley.

The men that Rand had left with him were the scum of the town, those with no love for the law. Joe and Freddy Phail were among them, along with others a lot worse. When the heat of the battle was on, Charley knew none of Rand's men would listen to orders from the marshal they so disliked. He had to admit he had given many of them reason to dislike him; those with no respect for the law had never received any respect from Charley Hanna.

When the defenses were completed Charley gathered the men for a solemn ceremony of straw-drawing. Some would have to fight in the street behind the barricades, others in the greater safety of the buildings. There had been a handful of volunteers for the outside duty—Charley and Bo among them—but the others decided to leave the decision to chance. When it was done there were ten men in all who would be given the job of fighting behind the makeshift breastworks that spanned the wide street; the others felt fortunate to have been spared the frontline task.

But even the buildings would not be safe, everyone realized. Especially if the Murphy gang really did have the powder from the gunsmithy.

Chapter 12

Noah Murphy chewed on the stub of a cigar as he watched his men rolling a keg of gunpowder over to a clearing in the snow outside the Redding cabin. It had taken a lot of daring to get the powder, right under the noses of the entire town, but Noah had managed to do it. Shifting the cigar stub from one side of his mustached lip to the other, the sandy-haired outlaw watched his men pry the lid off the keg, exposing the grayish powder within. Murphy smiled. Dry Creek wouldn't stand a chance now.

He had kept a close watch on the town from his post in the mountains. He knew of the town's fortifications, but they did not worry him. It would take more than a line of wagons, feed sacks, and barrels to stand up to the assault he had planned.

He wasn't certain whether Charley Hanna or the other two who had been with Willy before he died had any idea where the money was. It was only a remote possibility that Willy had talked before he died, but Noah had to assume he had. Otherwise there would be no hope of ever finding that cash. The men from Dry Creek who had tried had been fools. Dead fools now. Noah had enjoyed sending their ghastly parade into the center of town.

Until all of this had happened, Dry Creek had been just another town to Noah. But now he hated the place and everyone in it. Dry Creek had murdered Farril Royster, one of the few men Noah had regarded as a friend. And for that crime it would pay.

And besides, Noah always enjoyed burning a town. He hadn't done that in a while.

"We got it open, Noah. Now what are we going to do with it?"

Noah went to where the keg of powder

stood, several others beside it. Clamping his teeth down on his cigar butt, he smiled.

"Looks good, looks good. Phillip, hand me that empty bottle over yonder."

A young man in a checked shirt scurried to where a discarded whiskey bottle lay up against the side of a stump. He handed it to Noah.

"Now get me a piece of paper."

The young man disappeared into Sarah's empty house and came back with a page torn from a Bible. Noah rolled it into a funnel and inserted the small end into the mouth of the bottle.

"Now we start filling the bottle," Murphy said. He reached into the barrel and came up with a heaping handful of powder. Pouring it into the bottle, he repeated the action until the bottle was almost full. Then he reached to the ground and picked up a stick with a blunt end.

"Now we pack it down," he said, extending the stick into the bottle. He began probing and pounding into the powder, packing it in until it was tightly compressed in the glass.

"Do you have any of those fuses left from the Denver job?" he asked one of his men. A fat, red-headed man grunted and went to a saddle that lay across the top rail of a fence. Digging into one of the saddle bags, he pulled out a thick roll of fuse.

"Got more than I thought," he said.

"Fine. It'll come in handy. Cut me off some and stick it down in the bottle."

The man complied. Noah thrust the end of the fuse deep into the powder, then reached down and began gathering small pebbles, which he dropped into the bottle along with occasional pinches of powder. When the bottle was full, he packed the contents as tightly as he could once more. Then he held up the bottle with a smile.

"And here we have what's going to blow Dry Creek off the map," he said.

Every moment that passed only increased the tension in the air at Dry Creek. It was a town that waited. Commerce had stopped; men with rifles in their hands watched the hills, wondering when the attack would come. The morning sun climbed high and crossed the crest of the heavens, beginning a westward descent that marked the hours until the moment the town dreaded.

The women and children, along with the infirm and old, had been sent again to the back rooms of the Ketchum Boarding House

129

to wait until it was over. Though it was still early in the afternoon, Charley didn't trust Noah to wait until nightfall. In a way he almost hoped the outlaw would attack early just to relieve the awful tension of waiting.

Rand had assembled his men in the Lodgepole; some of them were on the roof of the building, keeping watch over the road leading from the mountains to the town. Charley was glad they were being so attentive and taking the attack seriously, but the more he looked at the group, the more a nagging worry ate at his mind.

All of the men Rand controlled were town troublemakers; each had at one time or another spent a night in jail, courtesy of Charley Hanna. Some had even voiced threats against the marshal. That had never greatly bothered Charley before, for drunks and scoundrels were always quicker with words than with action, but in the situation of battle he wasn't sure how cooperative those men would be with the rest of the fighters. And there was always the remote possibility that one of them might use the confusion of battle as a cover for a quick shot at the marshal himself.

That was a thought that had passed only quickly through Charley's mind, but passing though it was, it bothered him. Still, there was nothing he could do to protect himself against that possibility, so he forced himself not to worry about it.

It was almost two o'clock before he found time for his midday meal. He headed over to the jailhouse to fry up a few strips of bacon, trying to recall as he walked across the street whether or not he had eaten that last can of beans.

He opened the jailhouse door and was startled to see Sarah leaning over the stove, stirring a pot of stew.

"Sarah! When did you come in here?"

The slender young lady turned and smiled at the marshal. "A little while ago. I knew you would be too busy to fix anything yourself. Sit down. This is almost ready."

Charley grinned, tossing his hat to the peg on the wall. "You know, I should thrash you for being here. I told you to get into the boarding house with the others."

"Hush. You aren't going to thrash anybody. Now sit down like I told you and get ready to eat this while it's hot," she said, carrying a bowl of the hot stew to the desk, where Charley now sat. "I'll get you some coffee in just a second, and here's some biscuits."

Charley smiled. "I didn't expect such a feast. Sit down and join me, would you?"

She shrugged. "Why not? I could use a good meal."

The pair set in to the stew as if they hadn't eaten in a week. Sarah had done a good job—seasoning the stew just like Charley liked it—and before they realized it they had eaten the entire potful. Charley took his last scrap of biscuit and sopped up the remaining traces of stew on his tin plate.

"Mighty good, Sarah. Mighty good."

"I'm glad you thought so. It's been a long time since I've cooked for a man."

As Sarah made her last statement, a trace of sadness momentarily came over her. Her eyes clouded, and for an instant her thoughts were of her dead husband.

Charley saw it, surmised her thoughts, and felt an unexpected jolt of jealousy, followed immediately by guilt. He frowned. The feelings running through him were confusing. Sarah looked up at him; her eyes cleared, and it was as if she had returned. Charley felt a strange and profound relief.

"I'm glad you liked the meal," Sarah repeated.

"Best I've had in months. And a good break from all this tension."

Sarah nodded philosophically. "I know what you mean. It kind of gets to a person after a while, doesn't it? I mean, in the last couple of days I've felt like— Oh, but listen to me. It isn't me who's had problems, it's you. I've got no right to complain. I'm sorry."

"No, no, don't be. It's been hard on all of us. And until this is over things are just going to get more that way. It's just now sinking in to some of the folks here that the town is going to be attacked. It's not just a bad dream—it's real. God knows I wish it wasn't."

Sarah smiled weakly. When she spoke, her voice was low.

"Charley, I appreciate all you've done for me over these last few days. I don't know what I would have done if you hadn't been helping me out."

Charley appeared almost embarrassed by her words. "I've done nothing but my job."

Her voice was soft. "Is that all?"

Charley paused. "No."

He stood. "These last few days have drawn me close to you in a way different than anything I've ever felt for a woman. I'm no good at this kind of talk. What I'm trying

133

to say is that I think I'm falling in love with you."

Sarah silently watched Charley, who stood with his back toward her. Rising, she moved toward him.

"Do you think I haven't known? The times you've put your arm around me these last days, the way you protected me . . . I've known how you felt."

Charley turned and looked into her face. "And how do you feel, Sarah? Can I dare to hope you might love me?"

Sarah smiled. "Is there any way I couldn't?"

Charley drew her to him and kissed her.

Chapter 13

Night fell on Dry Creek. Still the town waited. No movement in the hills, no hint of coming danger. The street was lit with torches; men roamed about in it, rifles in hands. Most were smoking; all were nervous. In spite of the low temperature many of the waiting defenders of the town had to continually wipe beads of sweat from their brows.

Charley was among those on the street,

and he paced back and forth restlessly. All that could be done in preparation for the expected attack had been done. Riflemen watched the torchlit scene below them from the windows of the boarding house and the Mansfield Saloon; Rand's men did the same from the roof of the Lodgepole. Others were inside the log saloon. Rand himself gripped a Winchester at a small window near the corner of the building.

The younger men of the town had been given the task of guarding the alleyways through which the Murphy gang might find entrance, should they make it past the other defenders of the rears of the buildings. The narrow alleys were packed with anything that might stop a bullet, and the young men crouched behind the barricades with pale faces and trembling fingers wrapped around the stocks of their rifles. Many times the youths had talked of the countless tales of battle and life-and-death conflicts that had made up the history of the West. But now the excitement was gone, replaced by overwhelming dread and a sincere fear that they might not be alive to see the morning.

Dr. Hopkins was in the boarding house with the rest of the townspeople. He knew that once the battle began he would have plenty to do. He kept his black bag close beside his feet, and in a clean cloth sack beside him were heaps of fresh, clean bandages ready for use.

Preacher Bartlett moved about, giving words of encouragement to distraught women who had husbands and sons out on the street or in one of the buildings. But there was little he could do but express hope or breathe a short prayer with those who desired it.

Old men with pale eyes and hollow faces stirred restlessly, looking back on days when they had been younger, knowing that a few years before they would have been among the men out on the street. For many of them it was a time of conflicting feelings. They coveted the safety of this back room, yet also felt the urge to join the younger men of the town in defending those they loved.

Sarah fidgeted in her seat in the boarding house, longing to be near Charley. The knowledge that he loved her thrilled her, yet fear for his survival tormented her. She squeezed her eyes shut and hoped that Charley would be spared in the coming battle.

An hour passed after the darkness had fully settled in, but still there was no sign of an attack. Out on the street Bo Myers came to Charley's side. "Do you think maybe they gave up the idea?"

The marshal shook his head slowly. "There's hardly a thing in this world I wouldn't give if I thought that could be true," he said. "But I can't believe they would back out on the fight. Not after all they've done."

"I had just hoped maybe––"

"I know the feeling, Bo. Maybe they have backed out. But I wouldn't bet on it."

Martin Arlo stepped from the door of the Mansfield Saloon and walked over to where the pair stood. "Everything is ready in there, or at least as ready as it ever will be. In fact, everybody's getting a little restless."

"Tell them to be patient. They'll have action soon enough, I'll wager."

"What's Rand up to? Giving any trouble?"

Charley glanced toward the Lodgepole. "Ain't heard a peep out of him since dark. I reckon he's ready to fight along with all of us. I just hope he has the sense to give the right orders. Once this fight starts I don't figure them boys of his will be listening to me."

The three turned and looked down the street. The eerie flicker of the torches illuminated the stretch of dirt to the edge of town where the feeble light faded into darkness. It was a thick darkness that could hide a large band of men.

A glowing thing that fizzled and sputtered came arcing through the darkness. It flew almost to the barricade, and when it struck the ground and rolled to a stop Charley found himself staring numbly at a bottle well-stuffed with gunpowder, the fuse fizzling down to the last inch. For an instant his muscles seemed frozen and rigid, then at the last possible second he broke through his paralysis and flung himself directly into Arlo, simultaneously grabbing Bo with his free hand. The trio fell to the dirt as a tremendous blast plowed up the street, kicking dirt and broken glass everywhere, shaking but not breaking the barricade.

Arlo had fallen onto his back, and he stared upward to see a rain of dirt and grit pouring down toward him. He opened his mouth to scream, but his mouth filled with dirt and gravel, muffling his yell. He spat it out, choking.

From the darkness at the end of the street, bursts of light erupted, the roar of the gunfire echoing from the sides of the buildings. The siege of Dry Creek had begun.

Charley leapt to his feet, but crouched to keep his head below the top of the barricade. Bo picked himself up, dusting off his clothing and looking stunned. Men rushed to the barricade, thrusting rifle muzzles over the heaped-up furniture, feed sacks, and overturned wagons.

The roaring of gunfire filled the streets, masking the shouts of the men crouching behind the barricades and the cries of the townspeople hidden in the back room of the boarding house. Bullets smashed into the barricade; dirt was kicked up in the street from shots that struck short.

Charley rose to peer over the edge of a wagon resting on its side before him with dirt and rock heaped against its bed to stop the bullets that ripped through the wood. He caught sight of a flash of fire from the edge of the old deserted livery out beyond the barricade and sent a responding bullet winging toward the spot.

He ducked again and looked around him. All along the length of the barricade men were pouring a hail of lead toward the dark end of the street where the Murphy gang was hidden. From the windows of the Ketchum Boarding House rifle muzzles protruded, belching fire and smoke. Bullets sang into the night.

From atop the Lodgepole other rifles flared. Charley saw Joe Phail near the west end of the flat roof, squinting down the muzzle of his rifle. There was a sudden burst of fire from the livery at the end of the street, and Joe's hat flipped from his head and fell to the street. The young man flattened on his belly behind the raised front wall extending two feet above the level of the roof, suddenly aware of how close he had come to taking a bullet in the head.

Charley rose back up against the wagon and sent two more shots down toward the livery. In the lightning flashes of fire on the dark street he made out the quickly moving forms of men—just how many, he couldn't tell. Noah Murphy was said to lead a large group, and from the strength of the volley pouring in from the darkness Charley was sure those rumors were true.

The bottle bomb had confirmed his fear that the Murphy gang had the powder from the gunsmithy. With powder at their disposal, the gang could cause more trouble than the town was prepared to handle.

Bo scrambled to Charley's side. "Charley, if they hit this barricade—"

"There ain't much we can do, Bo. Whoa! Here comes another one!"

A whiskey bottle arched through the darkness, landing about twenty feet from the barricade. Almost before he thought, Charley stood upright, dangerously exposing his head and torso above the line of the barricade, aimed his rifle, and squeezed the trigger.

The slug hit the bottle squarely, shattering it and sending powder in all directions. When the burning fuse lit it there was no explosion, only the flaring of the powder, illuminating the street all around. Charley ducked back down, grinning.

"There's one that didn't blow," he said.

They heard a loud cry. The marshal jerked his head around to find where it had come from and caught sight of one of Rand's men pitching forward from the Lodgepole roof to sprawl out in the snow on the wrong side of the barricade. Charley thought at first the man was dead, but then he moaned and moved slightly.

"He's alive," said Charley. "Bo . . . go get Dr. Hopkins, quick!"

The deputy scurried off toward the boarding house, keeping his head low. Charley braced himself to leap over the wagon and race toward the wounded man, but Arlo's hand gripped his shoulder.

"No, Charley—let me do it."

And before Charley could stop him, Arlo vaulted the barricade and raced toward the fallen man. Charley stood transfixed for a moment, stunned by Arlo's sudden action, then noted increased fire from the Murphy gang's end of the street. The dirt at Arlo's heels began kicking up.

"Keep him covered!" shouted Charley. "Pour it on!"

Charley stood and fired toward the end of the street. All along the barricade others did the same, and those on the roof of the Lodgepole and in the second-story windows on the facing side added their own fire to the protective effort.

The fusillade of Murphy gang gunfire snuffed out suddenly. The outlaws obviously had ducked for cover in response to the sudden outpour of bullets. Arlo was now at the side of the fallen man, kneeling and looking at his wound—an ugly, bleeding chest wound that had punctured the lung.

"Move your butt, Arlo!" shouted Charley. "Don't sit there gawking!"

Arlo slipped one hand beneath the wounded man's knees, the other beneath his shoulders. As gently as he could, he picked him up and moved, more slowly this time, toward the barricade. Charley stood and took the wounded man from Arlo, then went gingerly but carefully toward the boarding house. Arlo scrambled to safety just as Dr. Hopkins came to the door of the boarding house with Bo just behind him. The gunfire ceased as suddenly as it had begun, and for a moment the town was engulfed in an eerie silence.

"Move him in here," Doc ordered. "Lay him on the couch."

Outside there was a horrific, tremendous blasting noise, and the building shook suddenly. Charley almost lost his balance as he carried the wounded man to the couch.

"What now?" he muttered, laying the man down. He dashed toward the door, followed by Bo.

A portion of the barricade had been blown away. Several of the men who had been fighting behind it were desperately trying to patch it, gathering up feed sacks with half of the contents blown out, piecing together the wall of furniture, some of which now was blown into huge splinters. The Murphy gang was taking advantage of the confusion, pouring a harder rain of fire upon the defenders.

Charley ran toward the gap in the barricade, ready to help rebuild it as best he could. But another bottle came arcing through the night and fell in the midst of the men.

"Clear out! Out!" Charley cried, leaping toward the bottle.

His fingers closed around it and he cast it back over the barricade just as the fuse burned to the powder. The blast sent glass flying in all directions. The concussion shattered the glass in the windows of the jailhouse office.

"Boys, in case you didn't know it, that was a close one," Charley said. "Way too close."

The men moved again to rebuild the barricade, keeping their heads low to avoid the bullets that whizzed above them. Meanwhile the men in the second-story windows and atop the Lodgepole kept on shooting toward the livery, where the Murphy gang was.

Another bottle flew over the barricade, landing not five feet from Charley. The marshal dropped his rifle and dodged toward the bottle, but before he could reach it something leapt in front of him, knocking him aside.

It was Bo. The young deputy grabbed the

bottle, but he did not throw it back over the barricade as Charley had done. Instead he grasped the burning fuse and yanked it out of the bottle. He stamped out the flare beneath his boot.

Charley smiled. "Good thinking, Bo. Now maybe we can turn some of their tactics against them."

Bo picked up the burned-out fuse and worked it back into the bottle, using a splinter of the shattered barricade to pack the powder tight again. "Let's just hold this until we can return it to Murphy and his boys," he said, slipping the bottle—a flat, flask-style whiskey container—into his coat pocket.

In the dark livery, Noah frowned. Around him his men fired toward the barricade and also sent shots toward the men who bobbed up on the roof of the Lodgepole Saloon or in the windows in the building across the street. But so far their shots had done little good. They had dropped only one man, as best he could tell. Even the powder-packed bottles had not had the effect Noah had hoped they would.

"Stop your shooting!" he yelled.

His men obeyed, but looked at him with expressions of puzzlement.

"We ain't doing much good turkey shooting like this," he said. "I got a better idea."

He walked back to the rear of the livery, where kegs of stolen gunpowder stood.

"Help me with this," he ordered one of his men. He pried off a keg's lid and poured about half the powder into another keg. He then began packing stones, stray nails, and pieces of broken bottle into the keg, mixing it throughout the powder.

"Go get me that nag of yours, Phillip," Noah said.

The man to whom he had spoken frowned, surmising what Noah had in mind. "Noah, that nag ain't much, but she was given me by my brother."

"And she's dragged us down as long as you've trailed with us," Noah said. "Go get her or you can run this keg down there yourself."

The man looked angry, but obeyed. He left the stable by the rear and came back with an old mare trailing behind him. Noah was just finishing nailing the keg's lid back in place, this time with a long fuse running through a hole in it and deep into the powder.

"How fast you think that nag can run?" Noah asked.

"Not very," the man said, thinking to save the animal.

"Put some coal oil on the tail, then," Noah ordered. "Then get me some rope."

Down at the barricade, the silence from the livery was rousing speculation. "You think they've left?" Bo asked Charley.

"Kind of doubt it," Charley responded. "Keep your eye sharp. They may be changing positions."

"Every now and then I think I see something moving," Bo said. "There—look at that! A fire!"

"A torch, it looks like," Charley said. He and Bo had seen the same flash of yellow light through the slightly ajar livery door.

Suddenly the door burst open. An old mare, whinnying pitifully, bolted out of the door. Charley winced in sympathy for the animal, for he saw its tail was flaming. He swore beneath his breath at Noah, for cruelty to an animal was something that boiled Charley's blood. But then he saw something that chilled it as quickly.

An old saddle was cinched on the nag's back and a long rope was tied to the saddle horn. On the other end of the rope was a keg into which a burning fuse ran.

The pain-crazed mare veered this way and

that along the street, drawing closer to the barricade all the while.

For a moment Charley seemed incapable of doing anything. This tactic was such a surprise that he couldn't think of a quick response. But suddenly Bo yelled, "Shoot it!" Charley snapped up his rifle.

He fired at the nag; Bo did too. Both missed, though the shots at least made the mare veer away from the barricade.

But it was too close, and the momentum of its run had the keg moving toward the barricade, with enough slack on the rope to bring it dangerously near before it stopped.

Someone on the Lodgepole roof shot the nag. It collapsed in a shivering heap. The keg rolled up close to the barricade. The fuse burned down to the keg lid, then through to the powder.

"Hit the ground!" Charley yelled.

Chapter 14

For a moment there was almost total silence in the town. Then came the blast.

It was spectacular, immense, deafening. Charley felt grit bury itself in his skin as if fired from a scattergun, felt the jolting shock of the explosion as it ripped across the street and the sudden rending of the barricade into a storm of splinters, dirt, and flying brick, and saw a body flip through the air like a rag doll in a tornado.

In the confusion Charley was conscious of the porch of the jailhouse collapsing and the right corner of the Mansfield Saloon being shredded into a huge, gaping hole. He heard men atop the Lodgepole Saloon crying out as bits of flying debris struck them, and a body pitched forward off the roof to flop into the snow. The barricade was half destroyed, the entire right end of it blown into pieces. In the boarding house people screamed, terror-struck by the blast, and mingled with their voice came the more muffled cries of the women in the back rooms.

Charley was stunned; he had struck his head against the corner of a barrel as he fell. Everywhere there was smoke, choking and stinging, and Charley found himself so addled he couldn't even rise.

Something struck the ground beside him —a bottle, filled with powder, the fuse fizzling horrifyingly close to the dark grains. For a moment he stared blankly at it, hardly able to focus his eyes. Then he forced his hand outward and it closed numbly around the bottle. He threw it blindly over the barricade just as the fuse burned all the way down.

The bottle exploded before it struck the ground. The flash lit the street and the roar echoed down the row of buildings. Almost simultaneously there was another rending blast, this one on the other side of the barricade. Bits of shattered furniture, ruptured feed sacks, and a wagon wheel flew into the air. Three men, staggered by the earlier blast of the barrel and leaning up against the barricade, were knocked backward by the explosion. Charley pushed himself up to look at the results. The barricade was almost totally gone now, a weak, scattered remnant of what it had been before, and the men who had been knocked back just now were lying too still for Charley's comfort.

He heard horses racing toward the barricade and a renewed clatter of blasting rifles filled the air. Charley glanced over the barricade portion that was left in front of him, then ducked down quickly.

A horse and rider leapt over him, the rear hooves of the animal scarcely clearing him. Two other riders galloped down the street in the confusion and sea of smoke, and Charley saw flaring bottles in their hands. He groped for his pistol just as the first rider heaved his bomb through a window in the Ketchum Boarding House. The others tossed their bottles through the windows of the Mansfield Saloon.

Charley fired his pistol almost blindly as the front wall of the Mansfield buckled outward from the force of the blast, and when he opened his eyes he saw a riderless horse loping down the street. But the other two riders had wheeled their mounts and were loping straight back toward the stunned defenders at the shattered barricade once more, this time with their pistols drawn.

Charley rolled to one side to escape being pounded by a horse that ran straight at him, and he fired a quick and useless shot at the rider, who returned the fire. But his shot also missed, and the rider passed Charley, riding through a gap in the barricade.

Charley climbed to his feet, then moved in a stoop toward the three men who lay where they had fallen after the earlier-tossed bottle had exploded in their faces. He heard more gunfire, for the Murphy gang was doing its best to pick off the men in the street. Already most had darted over to the Ketchum Boarding House, which remained intact, because the bottle bomb tossed through its window had not worked properly, merely flaring out without exploding.

Charley knelt beside one man, and Arlo, pale-faced and trembling, crouched beside him.

"He's in a bad way, Martin. You carry him in. . . . I'll check the others."

Arlo put his hands under the man's arms, lifting him as gently as possible by the armpits and dragging him toward the Ketchum Boarding House. To take him to the saloon would be almost useless, for though the building was closer, much of the front wall was gone, spread across the street, and most of the men who had been stationed there had apparently either been stunned or knocked completely out. Arlo feared, as he dragged the wounded man toward the boarding house, that a few might have been killed.

Charley darted up beside Arlo just as Arlo dragged the wounded man inside the boarding house door. A bullet smacked into the doorjamb beside Charley's head. He ducked.

"There's nothing to do for the others," he said. "They didn't survive it."

Dr. Hopkins came over from the couch against the opposite wall, where the wounded man put there earlier still lay, his chest tightly bandaged and his face gray as death. But he was breathing, and for now that would have to do. Dr. Hopkins had others to tend to.

"Where do you want this one, Doctor?"

"Yonder on that blanket."

Arlo transferred the man while Charley reloaded his pistol. He was worrying about the men next door in the Mansfield Saloon, for the blasts that had ripped through the building had been devastating. Charley feared the worst. There were now hardly any shots being fired from the building, and even the men on the second floor were in no good position to fight, for the blasts had kicked out most of the support of the second floor and it sagged badly. It was so weakened toward the front of the building that the men on it could not draw close enough to the windows to fire, for fear their weight would break the floor beneath them.

Charley dropped his pistol into his holster and moved toward the front door, preparing to dart around and enter the Mansfield Saloon. He moved over to the open door, peered cautiously around it, then moved.

Sarah Redding watched him from her position at the door of the rear kitchen of the boarding house. She glanced at Dr. Hopkins, whose shirt and vest now were bespeckled with blood.

Charley moved along the boardwalk, almost tripping over a piece of the saloon wall that had buckled out across his path. He saw from the corner of his eyes the flashing of rifle fire from the livery. Slugs smacked into the porch column beside him.

He darted into the shell of the Mansfield Saloon. He was shocked by what he saw.

The place was a heap of rubble. The men that were capable of fighting had moved toward the front of the building and were crouching behind whatever cover was available. Many others lay scattered about, some wounded, some obviously dead. Rage gripped Charley. So far Murphy and his gang had managed to do more damage in a few minutes than he would have anticipated they could do in several hours. All because of that powder.

"Bo!"

"I'm here, Charley."

The deputy came around the corner from the alley between the damaged jailhouse and the saloon, leaping into the frontless building before the Murphy gang had time to pin down their aim at him. In the confusion of the last minutes Charley had lost track of his deputy.

"Charley, that powder is killing us."

"You still got that bottle of powder you snatched?"

"Yeah. What you got in mind?"

Charley didn't get a chance to answer, for there was a sudden new intensity in the chattering of rifle fire from the top of the Lodgepole. Charley headed for the corner of the building, realizing then that he had dropped his rifle outside and had neglected to pick it up in the confusion. Quickly he drew his pistol.

The deputy suddenly moved forward, scooping up something off the boardwalk. A bullet thunked into the boardwalk at his feet as he moved back in, his fingers pinching at something.

"Got another one, Charley! Got another one!" Bo proudly held up another powder-filled bottle, the fuse snuffed out by his fingers just above the mouth of the bottle.

"Good job, Bo!"

"That makes two. Might come in handy."

They heard a single rifle firing, fast and desperately. Charley drew his pistol and began moving toward the front of the building, cutting around to the left, at the same time barking an order at some of the men around him.

"Come with me—we got trouble!"

Three men followed Charley around the front of the boarding house and toward the alley between it and the next building. They met a frightened young man coming out of the alley. Charley stopped him.

A pale face stared up into Charley's eyes. "They're coming through the alley. . . ."

Charley shoved the young man aside and leapt directly in front of the alley. A man was clambering up onto the barricade that blocked it. Charley fired and hit. The man fell back. Charley heard someone behind the man grunt as the body struck him. The marshal leapt to the side, concealing himself behind the corner of the adjoining building, motioning for the others to stay clear of the alley entrance.

More fire came from the old livery. Charley hunkered down to avoid being struck by the bullets that slapped the wall above him.

"They split up!" one of the men exclaimed. "We're trapped in the open!"

The men broke and ran. Charley shouted for them to keep their heads, but in the confusion of battle such direction was useless. The men scattered to various points all along the other side of the street, making them safe for a time from the gunfire from the livery, but also clearing the way for the members of the Murphy gang who were trying to enter the alley.

Charley dropped to his belly and rolled to fire a quick shot into the alleyway at the men who once more were attempting to clamber over the barricade. He rolled back quickly as a bullet struck the dirt at his side, then rose and ran at a crouch back toward the boarding house. It was no use remaining where he was; Murphy's men had free access now through the alley, and to try to stop them alone would be suicide.

He darted through the boarding house door, into a room filled with wounded men and pale women who were attempting to help Dr. Hopkins as he made his rounds around the makeshift hospital. A few of the men who had been fighting earlier behind the barricade now were crouched at the windows, peering out toward the Murphy gang, wanting to fire but fearing they might draw return fire that could be devastating to the doctor's efforts to help the wounded.

Charley could hear Murphy's men mounting the barricade in the alley beside the building. On impulse, he raised the muzzle of his pistol to the wall and fired a blind shot directly through the side of the building.

He heard the grunt of a man on the other side and knew his shot had struck home. There was rifle fire directly overhead, and there were further shots from the alley.

Charley paused, then his face broke into a smile. He darted toward the back stairs, racing up them and into the second-floor hallway. He glanced down the length of the hall and saw the wooden ladder that led through a ceiling doorway onto the roof. The door was open.

Charley climbed the ladder and peered out until he caught sight of Bo kneeling at the edge of the building, firing his rifle downward. The deputy would fire a shot, pull back as he avoided the return fire, lever another shell into his rifle chamber, and fire once more.

Charley raced to the deputy's side and glanced into the dark alley. The last of Murphy's men were moving out of the rear of the alleyway as quickly as they could, their plan to mount the barricade forgotten. The sudden appearance of Bo on the rooftoop had provided an effective deterrent against any further action, and the crumpled bodies lying across the barricade and in the dirt behind it were ample evidence of the devastation the young deputy had rendered.

Two remaining Murphy gang gunmen darted back toward an old log shed that backed up the building just across the alley, and after they had pushed inside, a volley of slugs winged out over Charley's head. The marshal and his deputy dropped to their bellies on the flat roof. Increased shooting from the street behind them let them know that the battle there had increased in intensity.

Charley saw Bo fumbling in his pocket. The deputy produced one of the bottles he had intercepted. Charley dug in his pocket for the matches he always carried, and he shoved them over to Bo.

The deputy struck the match against the edge of the roof, shielding the flame with the palm of his other hand. He glanced at Charley. "Wish me luck!" And he lit the short fuse.

There wasn't time to move carefully, for the fuse was almost burned down to the powder by the time Bo had flipped the match away. Without regard to the bullets whistling around him, Bo rose and threw the bottle toward the shed that held the gunmen.

The bottle struck the wall of the shed just above the single open window of the crude structure, then fell to balance precariously on the sill before tipping backward into the little building.

Bo dropped to his belly just as the bottle exploded, gutting the flimsy shed. Bits of wood flew high into the air behind the building, and snow and splinters rained down on the marshal and his deputy.

Charley raised his head and shook the dirt from his hair. The shooting in the main street behind them had stopped. The stillness of the night was so intense that it almost roared in his ears.

"Bo . . . do you think . . ."

They moved across the roof and peered over the raised front of the building to the street. There was no more gunfire erupting from the old livery. The men atop the Lodgepole sat in vigil, their rifles gripped tightly. The street, torchlit and strewn with rubble and occasional bodies, was silent.

The first round of the Murphy gang siege was over. Charley sighed and sank to his haunches, listening to his loudly beating heart.

Chapter 15

The town fell into a strange combination of relief and despair. A few men ventured into the street to gather the bodies of the dead. The horror had taken its toll on all, and the wails of those who had lost husbands, sons, and brothers in the fight rose all around.

Charley, relieved though he was that the siege was at least temporarily stopped, did not suppose it was over. Just why Noah had chosen to withdraw, Charley wasn't certain; perhaps it was because the attempt to send part of his men into town through the alleys had failed, or maybe he simply didn't like his fighting position. Charley suspected that the withdrawal from battle would lead to an even more deadly attack as soon as the outlaw could develop some further scheme.

Based on the amount of powder that had been stolen from the gunsmithy, Charley was sure Murphy had more on hand. It was the gunpowder that was destroying the town, for the defenders had nothing of equal power to throw back. The destruction of the barricade had shown how quickly the Murphy gang could overthrow what feeble defenses the town could construct. Charley considered ordering the barricade rebuilt, but decided against it. What the Murphys had done once, they could do again, and it might be better to spend the time refortifying the buildings rather than trying to gather together the shattered remnants of the barricade.

Charley walked into the boarding house to see how Dr. Hopkins was doing with the wounded. He found the front room of the house even more crowded than it had been before, for several of the men who had suffered slight wounds had come in to have them patched.

"How's it going, Dr. Hopkins?"

The old man glanced irritably at the marshal. "How do you think? Leave me alone. I got no time to waste."

The old doctor moved away, and Charley lifted his brows. The old codger was irritable enough, but he had good reason. Charley could see that he was doing as well as he could with the wounded, and so left him to his work.

Sarah approached. She looked frightened, but also happy to see Charley. He turned to her and opened his arms, and she rushed into his embrace. He squeezed her close, stroked her hair with his rugged hand.

"Is it over, Charley?"

"For a while. But they'll be back."

Sarah looked despairing. "I hoped they had given up. Charley, I don't know how much more of this I can take."

Charley said, "Noah Murphy has got his heart set on burning the town. There's nothing we can do but fight it out to the end."

Sarah's face reddened, and she appeared almost angry. "But it's absurd! Is anything worth that?"

"It ain't a question of what's worth what. It's just a matter of what is."

Sarah looked away. "Is it that simple? Folks are going to die, and that's all there is to it?"

"I'm afraid so."

"I never thought it could be so bad. If I had I . . ." She trailed off, turned, and walked away. Charley watched her, puzzled. She seemed preoccupied and sad. He put it down to tension, forgot about it and went out into the street.

Rand watched the marshal through the small window at which he had remained throughout the battle. He had fired an occasional shot but for the most part had tried to stay as safe as he could without being too obvious about it. He had been as surprised by the abruptness of the initial attack as anyone else, and though he refused to admit it, had been very frightened throughout the fight. He didn't envy Charley's position out there on the street. He preferred to do his fighting behind thick walls.

The marshal disappeared into the ravaged saloon, and Rand turned and headed for the back door of the Lodgepole. He went out into the night, the crusty snow crunching beneath his feet, and began climbing the rough ladder set up against the back of the building.

He mounted the roof to be greeted by dark stares from the men shivering in the wind that whistled down from the mountains and skirted across the flat rooftop. He walked past most of them, heading for where Joe Phail sat crouched in the corner, his Winchester '73 across his knees.

"Hello, Joe. Where's your brother?"

The young man gestured over the edge of the roof. Rand glanced over and saw a body crumpled against a feedbag that had been a part of the barricade. It was Freddy Phail. Rand shuddered.

"What happened?"

"He got shot just after that keg of powder

blew the barricade up," Joe said. "Shot blew him clean off the roof."

"Sorry."

Joe nodded. "I'm going to make Murphy's boys sorry, too, if it's the last thing I ever do. Freddy never hurt nobody."

"Yeah."

Rand looked away from Joe toward the saloon. The young man caught a pondering look in his eye.

"Is something else wrong?"

The gambler glanced back at the young man, his expression contemplative. After a pause he said, "Can I trust you not to tell anyone about what I'm going to tell you?"

Joe looked at him intently, his grief over the loss of his brother giving way a bit to curiosity. "Sure, Rand. I can keep a secret."

The gambler placed his hand on the young man's shoulder and pulled him close. He spoke to him quietly, inches from his ear.

"Your brother and I had a deal, Joe. Something I discussed with him before the Murphy gang showed up. And now that he's gone, it hurts my plan."

"What plan?"

Rand gazed sternly at Joe, making a final evaluation. He again asked if he could trust him to keep a secret. Joe once again assured him he could.

"And will you do something for me if I ask you—and pay you well for it?"

The young man looked confused. "What are you talking about?"

Rand hesitated, then began to rise. "Forget it, Joe."

"No! I'll do it, whatever it is. Just tell me."

Rand smiled. "Very well, then. I'm giving you the job I had given your brother. I want you to do something for me while the fighting goes on . . . to make sure of something."

"What's that?"

"I want you to make certain Charley Hanna doesn't survive. Shoot him down, just like your brother shot down Farril Royster—without being detected."

An hour passed without sign of further attack. Charley regrouped the men under his control and new plans for defense were drawn up. With the barricade destroyed there was now no way to keep the Murphy gang out of the main street. The defenders would have to count on careful shooting to keep the town from being overrun.

But Charley worried that with the Murphy

gang still in possession of the gunpowder there would be little to do against them. One well-placed explosion in the already damaged saloon could wipe out the building. One in the boarding house might kill many of the townsfolk hiding there, as well as the wounded whom Dr. Hopkins was tending. Only by the most daring, accurate shooting possible could the town defenders hope to effectively counter the attack.

Sarah had returned to the back room of the boarding house, where she had gone after her talk with Charley, and now she paced nervously about, her movements watched with disinterest by most of those who kept their nervous vigil there, but with much interest by Kathy. Kathy had been watching Sarah much of the time over the last hours, her anger growing all the while. She pondered how Sarah had taken the man Kathy secretly loved away from her, and the thought nagged at her until she could hardly bear it. Kathy felt compelled to stare at Sarah, her feelings smoldering inside.

Yet at the same time Kathy felt guilty because of the lies she had spread about Charley. Ever since her last talk with Rand she had been determined to keep things as they were, but still she knew what she had done was wrong.

Kathy had never before been a jealous individual, not until she had seen Charley slipping away from her. In her heart she knew he had never been hers in the first place, but before there had always been a hope that perhaps one day he would be. Now the hope was gone, and Kathy resented it.

Sarah was standing near the doorway of the room, her arms folded in front of her. As Kathy stared at her, Sarah suddenly stepped through the doorway and out toward the front of the building, walking with a determined stride.

Kathy frowned. What was she up to? According to Charley's orders, all the townsfolk who weren't fighting, helping with the wounded, or loading weapons for the fighters were supposed to remain where they were. Kathy hesitated, then curiosity overwhelmed her, and she slipped out of the room after Sarah.

She saw Sarah weaving her way through the makeshift hospital in the main room of the boarding house, then she slipped out the front door. In the bustle and confusion no one seemed to notice, and when Kathy followed, no one stopped her, either.

Kathy looked slyly down the boardwalk. Sarah was heading toward the saloon, no more than a few yards ahead of her. Kathy ducked back into the shadows and watched as Sarah looked cautiously around the edge of the almost demolished building, peering into the room as if trying to avoid detection.

Strange, Kathy thought. She had assumed that Sarah had left the room in search of Charley, but it now appeared she was trying to avoid being spotted by him—or anyone else, for that matter. Why? Kathy was intrigued. She determined to follow Sarah farther.

Sarah moved quickly across the open front of the saloon, apparently making it without being seen by anyone on the inside, for no one tried to stop her, as someone surely would have if she had been spotted. Kathy followed to the same point Sarah had been before, then peeped around the corner into the saloon. Torchlight flickered on her auburn hair and cast strange, dancing shadows on the smoke-blackened wall beside her.

The saloon was crowded with fighters. Kathy heard the clatter of rifles being loaded and pistols being checked. Faces turned almost toward her, and she ducked back. Glancing down the street, she saw Sarah mounting the boardwalk in front of the jail, moving past the shattered remnant of the barricade.

Now Kathy *was* confused. Sarah was heading toward the edge of town.

She glanced once more into the interior of the saloon. Still the men mingled about, many of them filling ammunition pouches or belts with slugs from several boxes being overseen by the gunsmith. She wasn't sure whether she could make it across the gap where the front wall had been without being seen, but she would try. Otherwise Sarah would be out of her sight and Kathy would never know the answer to the mystery that was tantalizing her.

She waited a few seconds longer, then darted across the gap. She tried to move swiftly, but not too swiftly, for a blur of motion might catch someone's attention. And with nerves on edge as they were, she might even be shot before she was recognized.

Amazingly enough, she made it. She entered an area of thick shadow at the corner of the jailhouse, and stood panting for a minute.

The men atop the Lodgepole! She had

forgotten them! They had a clear view of the street.

She glanced in that direction. No one was visible against the blackness of the sky. The men must have moved momentarily off their perch, or at least to the back section of the roof, probably to get fresh ammunition as the men in the Mansfield Saloon were doing.

She looked out into the darkness beyond the reach of the flickering torches that lined the street. Sarah had gone into that sea of shadows and for the moment was lost from sight. Kathy squinted, trying to see into the murk.

She caught sight of a fleeting figure, a skirt tossing. Kathy started forward in pursuit, then suddenly pulled to a stop.

Another figure was moving on the opposite side of the street, coming around from the rear of the Lodgepole. It was Rand Cantrell, and from the look of things he was heading into the darkness after Sarah.

Kathy felt a chill. In spite of the fact that Rand had provided her, in his willingness to do anything to hurt Charley Hanna, with a welcome tool of revenge against the man who had jilted her, Kathy knew Rand was evil. He could be planning nothing but wrong toward Sarah. Strangely, that thought made

Kathy feel suddenly protective toward the very lady she detested most.

She waited until Rand had moved on down the dark street after Sarah, then followed. She slipped as quietly as possible into a path almost directly behind Rand, who clearly had no idea he was being followed.

Sarah had reached the stable where the Murphy gang had been holed up. Bravely she approached the gaping doorway of the building, and Kathy held her breath in anticipation of a burst of gunfire from inside the structure. But it never came. The livery was, to all appearances, deserted.

Kathy paused, tense and breathless, and watched Sarah disappear inside. Rand paused at the edge of the door, probably worried about the possible presence of the outlaw band, but when nothing happened he entered after Sarah.

Kathy was shaking. She was drawn toward the stable, even though she also felt a strong urge to run back to safer confines. She stepped silently after Rand, into the darkness inside the empty livery.

Sarah stood in the livery, looking around, fear and confusion in her face. She stared into the dark, vacant stalls and peered upward to the black loft.

"Noah Murphy?"

Sarah's voice was soft. Kathy understood now what the young widow was doing. It was suddenly hard to hate her.

"Noah Murphy, are you here?" Sarah was trembling from more than the cold.

Movement in the shadows. Sarah wheeled around. "Is that you?"

A figure stepped from the darkness. "Not quite, Mrs. Redding."

Sarah recoiled at the sight of Rand. "What are you doing here? Why did you follow me?"

"Who wouldn't follow a young woman who so strangely heads straight for the pit of the viper, so to speak? What are *you* doing here?"

Sarah drew herself up straight. "Do you really want me to tell you?

"Indeed."

"I came to do what you've been wanting. I came to turn myself over to Noah Murphy."

Chapter 16

Rand laughed. "Noble of you, my lady! Such a spirit of self-sacrifice! But I'm afraid

I can't let you do this. I have other needs for you."

"What do you mean?" The young woman inched away from Rand, who suddenly seemed to stand several inches taller, looking very threatening.

"I'll be needing you later as a ticket out of town, if it comes to that." He touched his pistol. "Come with me."

Sarah backed away. "No!"

The pistol came out of the holster and was leveled at Sarah's abdomen. "I'm afraid you have no choice, Mrs. Redding. You're coming with me."

He lunged forward and his hand roughly gripped her shoulder. It wasn't a callused hand like most men's—the skin was that of a man who knew little real labor, a hand that spent more time delicately caressing a deck of cards than gripping a spade or swinging a pick—but it firmly gripped Sarah's feminine shoulder. With a cry the young widow was pulled into Rand's grasp.

"Let her go!"

Kathy stepped into view, startling the gambler and making him lose his grip on Sarah. The fleet young woman twisted away from him and half fell against the wall of an empty stall.

Rand glowered. "Where did you come from!"

"I followed you. This time I'm not playing your game. Don't you know we've done enough wrong already? I was a fool to listen to you. I won't let you do this—"

Rand's lips spread over two rows of even teeth, and his arm whipped back. The pistol descended and crashed against Kathy's skull. The auburn-haired lady let out a muffled cry and collapsed. Sarah tried to scream, but her voice failed her.

"Now you'll come with me," Rand said, moving forward, not taking even a glance at Kathy's form crumpled on the floor. He grasped Sarah's arm, pulling her to him. His pistol pressed her throat.

"If you make a sound, you'll regret it."

Sarah, trembling, stumbled along as Rand held her arm in a painful position. He stopped in the doorway and looked out across the street to see if he could proceed unseen. The pistol at her throat stifled Sarah's urge to shout to the men in the saloon and boarding house. Rand looked carefully all along the street, knowing that a careless move might expose him, although he counted on the thick darkness to mask him.

He bent and talked into Sarah's ear. "You

move along in front of me, real slow, doing nothing to draw attention. If you so much as make a wrong step and expose us, then I swear you'll take a bullet. That's an absolute guarantee. You understand?"

Sarah nodded quickly.

"Move on, then. Now."

The pair stepped out into the street, Rand holding Sarah closely, making it difficult for her to walk. As they progressed he half carried, half shoved her along, hugging close to the wall and staying in the shadows.

"We're going around toward the back of the Lodgepole. I don't want anyone to see us, not even my own men. You keep that in mind and you'll be all right."

He rounded the old livery and headed along the side of the adjacent building, cutting around the rear of the structure and toward the Lodgepole. Sarah could make out the form of a man on the rooftop, a rifle in his hands. But he appeared to be looking toward the main street, not noticing them as they moved carefully along in the darkness.

Standing in the rear of the Lodgepole was a small storage building made of narrow logs joined together in the style of a stockade or French log house. There was a stout pine door on the structure, standing ajar. Rand shoved Sarah toward the building.

"Get inside." He pushed her forward. She fell to her face in a sea of grime and greasy dirt. She looked back over her shoulder, trying to fight off tears.

Rand dug in his pocket and after a moment produced a padlock. He dangled it on his finger before her, smiling. "I came prepared, you see!" Then the pine door slammed shut, the noise of the lock closing on the latch filtered through it, and Sarah was left alone in the darkness.

She heard Rand moving away, and through a space between two of the upright logs she watched him go into the alley between the Lodgepole and the adjacent building. In moments he would be back inside the saloon, and no one would have any idea she was trapped here.

She could cry for help, of course, but the only men close enough to hear her would be Rand's men—or Rand himself. She could make no escape attempt without him finding out about it.

At least she was alive and unhurt.

But what of Kathy? She was mystified by Kathy's actions. Why the woman who before had stood so staunchly beside Rand would make such a sudden change she couldn't be sure. Before, Kathy had helped the gambler spread his lies; now she had risked her own life to keep him from hurting Sarah.

A ticket out of town, Rand had called Sarah. The implications of that were not clear. Why would he need a hostage? It implied that for some reason he might need protection when all of this was over. But why? There was something going on that made Sarah's skin crawl. She huddled back into the darkness and shivered in a numbed silence.

In the devastated saloon Charley had finished making his defense preparations. Rubble had been gathered and stacked in front of the building, and temporary props had been thrown up beneath the sagging portion of the upper floor. It was all very rickety and weak, and Charley knew that one explosion could blow it all away, but there was nothing more to be done.

The continued absence of the Murphy gang gave him more worry than comfort. He was smart enough to know that they weren't finished with the town and probably intended to let Dry Creek sweat awhile before renewing their attack.

He glanced toward the Lodgepole. Rand

was nowhere in sight; but then, he hadn't been, throughout the battle. At least his men had fought well, and all the previous stir over just who would give the orders seemed a bit pointless now. In the heat of the battle there had been little time to worry about such things, and Rand at least had stayed out of the way. Charley looked at the men seated above the roofline of the Lodgepole. Most were staring out into the darkness outside of town, waiting, just like everyone else. But he noticed one man—it looked like Joe Phail—staring back at him. When Charley frowned at him, Joe looked quickly away. Charley turned and promptly forgot the incident, seeing nothing of significance in it. But when his back was toward Joe, the young roughneck began staring at him again.

Charley went over to the boarding house once more to see how Dr. Hopkins was progressing. He found some of the wounded had been moved into the rear hallway, with Dr. Hopkins still probing for a bullet in one thin man who had taken a shot in the side. The old doctor was sweating and looking weary, and Charley knew better than to bother him. He went past him to the rear room, where the woman, children, and old ones were.

He stepped over a cot holding a pale man

who seemed to be hardly breathing, entered the room, and looked around.

"Where's Sarah?"

"She took out of here a while back. Kathy Denning went after her. Ain't seen either one of 'em since," a woman said.

Charley frowned. "Did they say where they were going?"

"No. Didn't ask."

Charley left the room. Sarah . . . leaving? Followed by Kathy? That worried him. It wasn't like Sarah to disobey orders, but she had left the room in strict violation of what he had directed. Fear raced through his mind; he felt a panicked desire to find Sarah as fast as he could.

Charley headed out into a darkness broken by the flickering light of the torches. A young man was replacing the torches that had burned out, and Charley touched his shoulder.

"Do you know Sarah Redding?"

"Yes sir."

"Have you seen her in the last few minutes?"

"No sir . . . I—"

He was interrupted by a sudden burst of shouts. Men ran in a panic through the mixture of mud and snow that made up the street, and Charley knew that the attack had resumed.

Men on horseback bolted through the darkness more suddenly than Charley would have anticipated, and as soon as they reached the edge of the circle of light cast by the torches, they began firing at the men who were frantically darting back behind the makeshift breastworks and barricades in front of the devastated saloon and in the alleys. By some miracle all of them made it, though the boy to whom Charley had been talking was clipped in the shoulder by a bullet.

Charley leapt headlong through the air and rolled to a landing in the alley between the saloon and boarding house. He had recovered his rifle from the street during the break in the fighting, and now he trained the sight on a man astride a horse making a graceful leap across the barricade on the opposite end of the street, a place where the fighting so far had scarcely touched. He squeezed the trigger; his eyes were blurred momentarily by the thick burst of gunsmoke. Through the white haze he saw the man throw his arms to the sky and pitch backward into the snow.

Charley headed for the saloon, but a bullet

clipped at his heels and he dropped back to his previous position, looking wildly around.

The bullet had come from the opposite side of the street. Charley looked toward the gunsmithy, a building that through the fight had remained empty. A fading puff of smoke hanging in front of the window of the dark building proved the place was empty no more.

Charley raised his rifle and blasted out a pane of glass, hoping his shot did some damage to the Murphy gang gunman inside.

But a rifle muzzle poked out through the broken pane and began spitting fire again. Another shattered the adjoining window and did the same. Charley dropped, then heard the noise of oncoming riders again.

Several horses leapt the blasted barricade and raced down the middle of the street. Charley fired, missed, but was happy to see that some of the defenders in the saloon beside him had better luck. Three riders pitched to the earth. One was trampled by the horses behind him; the others lay still as soon as they struck the ground.

But the riders who made it managed to pour a steady rain of bullets into the front of the saloon and along the roof of the Lodgepole. Charley saw Rand's men duck to escape the hail of bullets.

Charley used the cover of confusion to move toward the Mansfield Saloon. He ran swiftly along the few feet of boardwalk between him and his goal. Bullets erupted from somewhere to punch into the wall beside him and into the boardwalk at his feet.

He threw himself over the breastworks at the front of the building and rolled as he struck to break his fall. He came up beside Bo Myers.

"Somebody about plugged me that time, Bo. The Murphy gang . . ."

"It wasn't the Murphy gang, Charley. Those shots came from the Lodgepole! I saw it!"

"What?"

"Somebody at the Lodgepole just shot at you!"

Charley was stunned. Hardly thinking about the danger of exposure, he lifted his head and peered over the rubble that protected the fighters.

A bullet struck inches from his face, stinging and hot. He pulled quickly down. A shiver ran over him.

Bo was right. The shot had come from the Lodgepole.

"I never would have thought Rand would go this far. . . ."

A man near Charley rose and ran toward the other side of the building. A single blast of gunfire came from atop the Lodgepole; the man fell, grunting, with a painful shoulder wound. Quickly he scrambled for cover.

"It was Joe Phail who fired that shot!" Bo exclaimed.

"Are you sure?"

"Positive!"

Charley remembered his earlier fear that someone on Rand's side might use the battle as an excuse to rid themselves of a troublesome town marshal. He felt sure Joe's shot had been intended for him.

Atop the Lodgepole, one of the men wriggled over to Joe.

"What are you trying to do, Joe?"

Joe turned a frown on the man. "I'm doing a special favor for somebody, at their request."

The man chewed on his tongue, frowning. "You wouldn't be trying to shoot the marshal, would you?"

"None of your affair."

"Yes it is . . . because shooting the marshal is what Rand Cantrell is paying me to do!"

Joe realized then that Rand had covered himself from several angles, apparently having recruited more than one man for the same job. Rand obviously wanted Charley dead, and that Joe didn't fault him for. But he didn't like being double-dealed.

"You leave the marshal to me," Joe said.

"No can do. He's mine."

The man raised himself over the edge of the roof and fired a shot toward Charley. Bo saw it, exclaimed about it. Others saw it too, this time. Charley felt a wave of disgust at Rand, and concern for his own life. The men atop the Lodgepole were more likely than Noah's gang to do him damage.

"I'll not stand by and be shot at," Charley said, leveling off at the top of the Lodgepole. When Joe's head and shoulders appeared as the fellow prepared to try for Charley again, Charley fired. Joe disappeared, and Charley could tell from how he was knocked back that the bullet had connected and Joe was no longer a concern. The other man who had fired at him remained, though. Charley did not know who it was; he had not gotten a clear glimpse.

There . . . the man was there again, aiming down. . . .

This time it was Bo who fired first, and

Bo who connected. The man fell back behind the Lodgepole's false front.

"Thanks, Bo. There's two less to worry about," Charley said.

"Yeah," Bo returned. "But two less to fight the Murphy gang, too."

Chapter 17

Noah Murphy watched incredulously from the gunsmithy as the unexpected exchange of fire took place between the townfolk, who before had been united in fighting against him. Full of surprises, these folks were; they had fought a much harder fight than he had expected so far, and now they were taking on each other. He couldn't figure it out.

They had exacted a bitter toll on his gang, and that roused a mixture of feelings in Noah. The gang had grown too large—that he knew—and the loss of some of them wasn't a bad thing. He had sensed a growing rebelliousness in some of his men, and Noah had secretly hoped some of the more troublesome ones would be conveniently eliminated in this fight. But he had not anticipated the level of losses he had suffered so far. He had lost men he had hoped to lose, but also some he had hoped to keep.

He analyzed this new twist. With the town divided against itself, perhaps he could take even greater advantage. Most of his men were stationed at the opposite end of town from before, ready for what Noah hoped to be a final onslaught. The men were angry now, fired up, personally riled at Dry Creek for what it had done to their number. Noah figured his men would be ready to take risks to do the most damage to the town's defenders. Which suited Noah, whose goal was to put Dry Creek through as much misery as possible with a minimum of risk to himself.

He heard his men now, riding once more down the street, flashing past him, low in the saddle, with powder-filled bottles in their hands, fuses flaring.

Charley also saw the riders from his position in front of the Lodgepole and knew what was coming. At the last moment he fired his rifle at the lead rider, knocking him from the saddle just as he threw his hand bomb deep into the saloon. The other riders did the same. At the same time Bo lunged forward, but Charley could not see why he did.

The explosions ripped the saloon with devastating force, knocking what remained of the front wall into the street. The walls on either side fell, and bodies flipped out like leaves in wind. The concussion lifted Charley from the floor, then something heavy fell on top of him, and for a moment all was dark for him.

A pinpoint of light reached him. He stared at it, then realized he was looking through a gap in rubble that had fallen atop him. Beyond, he saw the street in front of the building.

Horses and riders lay about, as if kicked aside by an explosion in their midst. These were Murphy's men, Murphy's mounts. As Charley watched, a few of the downed men rose and ran. Gunfire from atop the Lodgepole dropped some; others got away. Charley did not have the impression they would return to fight.

Down the street more of Murphy's men rode as hard as they could go. From the slump of a couple of them, Charley saw they were wounded. He shook his head to clear it, and tried to figure out what had happened out there.

He remembered Bo's lunge forward just as the blasts came, and then he understood.

Bo had thrown his second recovered bomb into the midst of the riders at the same time they had thrown their own into the saloon. The explosion must have been horrific and perfectly timed, for it had done more to damage the Murphy gang than any single turn of the battle so far.

Charley struggled to free himself from the rubble that trapped him. He looked around as best his cramped situation would allow and heard moans from other men nearby. To his left he heard someone scrambling across the fallen timbers. The rubble around him creaked and moved, and he twisted his head to see Martin Arlo pulling the rugged beams and timber away.

"I'll have you out, Charley."

Arlo jerked and pitched forward onto the ground. Blood flowed from beneath him.

Charley pushed Arlo up and away and raised himself, trying to see if all his limbs still moved normally. Arlo groaned; thank God he was alive. Charley went for his pistol. He drew and fired one shot. A rifleman atop the Lodgepole spasmed and fell.

Still trying to kill me, Charley thought. Rand must have offered a reward for my death.

Charley crawled out atop the rubble, dragging Arlo by the shoulders to the rear of the heap of fallen ceiling timbers. Shots rained into the saloon, fired by Lodgepole gunmen, and Charley felt his shoulder burn as a shell winged past and peeled a line across his skin. He dropped to the grit-covered floor beside Arlo, then bobbed to fire another shot at the Lodgepole.

He heard shooting from the boarding house. The few gunmen stationed there apparently saw what the Lodgepole gunmen were about and were returning fire. Staccato rifle blasts also sounded further up the street, and Charley surmised that whoever of the Murphy gang was in the gunsmithy were also continuing their battle. Charley wondered how long that would go on, for the Murphy riders in the street who had been scattered by Bo's bomb were disappearing one by one, either being dropped or simply running away. Charley could spot only two or three who continued seriously to fight.

Several other men extricated themselves from beneath the rubble in front of Charley and ran, crawled, or dragged themselves to safer spots.

Charley thought fleetingly of Sarah. He wondered if she was safe, especially now that the fighting was so fierce.

Charley began to formulate a plan. It was time to end this battle. He looked down at Arlo. The man was pale and in pain, but the wound in his shoulder didn't look severe.

"Martin, I can't get you help with the fighting going so hard."

"I reckon I won't die, Charley."

"Glad to hear it. Got to go now."

Charley dodged out the back door of the saloon and along the back of the row of buildings, heading toward the church house.

He kept a close eye on the forests to his left as he moved, for he feared hidden Murphy gang fighters who might linger there unseen. But there was no movement inside the dark treeline, and Charley traveled swiftly without incident.

He passed the shattered hut into which Bo had cast his first bomb. In the dimness of the ruptured building he could see the bodies of men. Bo had done an efficient job. Charley remembered suddenly that the deputy had been beside him when the ceiling collapsed and had not emerged from the rubble to rejoin the fight. Was he dead? Charley hoped not, but he feared the worst.

Charley used the buildings and alley barricades for cover until he reached the snowy yard between the final building on the street and the church house, which sat back from the street several yards. He stopped long enough to empty the spent shells from his pistol cylinder and replace them with live ones.

He reholstered the pistol as he rounded the rear of the building, staying close to the wall. He moved in a catlike, stalking stance around the side of the building.

A barricade stretched out before him, un-damaged from any of the fighting, for most of that had been concentrated on the far end of the street. The Murphy riders had leapt it earlier in their final assault. Charley dropped to his knees in the snow and peered over the top of the breastworks.

The gunsmith shop was down about a hundred feet in the row of buildings across the street. As Charley had suspected, some Murphy fighters were still inside, for he saw the muzzles of two weapons protruding from the windows, sneezing flame and smoke.

He dropped to his belly and began wriggling forward in the snow. It chilled his skin and soaked his clothing. He proceeded with determination, keeping himself low.

It took him longer than he had anticipated to make it across, and when at last he crawled to safety on the side of a building there, he was winded from exertion.

He stood up, brushing the snow from his pants, and went toward the rear of the building. Once there, he drew his pistol and steeled his nerve.

Though he had seen evidence of only two, he didn't know exactly how many gunmen were in the gunsmithy. What he was about to do might accomplish nothing more than getting him killed. But then it just might also accomplish the final defeat of the Murphy gang . . . if he could preserve the element of surprise until the last moment.

He stepped forward, his boot crunching a little too loudly in the snow, making him wince. After a moment's pause he continued.

From this angle there was no visible sign of battle. Only the noise of gunshots gave evidence of the fight. Here in the safety of the backside of the buildings things were incongruously peaceful.

He moved further down the row until he reached the gunsmith shop. The rear door stood ajar, and inside Charley heard two men talking, along with the occasional sound of gunfire.

"Noah, I tell you, they're all dead or run out! We got to get out ourselves!"

Charley whistled silently in surprise. Noah Murphy himself was in there! The very man responsible for all of this. Charley felt a sudden morbid determination.

He stepped forward as carefully as he could. He moved to the open doorway and squinted as he peered inside.

The door opened onto the rear room of the building, from which another doorway led into the front room, where Noah and his companion were. Charley carefully stepped inside, his heart pounding.

Pausing to prepare himself, he moved forward another step. Just as his foot touched the floor, there was a sudden, unexpected break in the fighting, and in the moment of silence the sound of his footfall carried through the open doorway into the front room.

"What was that?" Noah's companion asked.

Charley rushed through the doorway, cocking back the hammer of his .44 at the same time. Noah's face went pale; his partner yelled as if stung, then leveled his rifle at Charley.

Charley squeezed the trigger of his pistol. The roar reverberated through the tiny room, shaking the walls. Noah's companion fell. As he did, Noah tossed aside his empty rifle with a roar of rage. His hand dropped swiftly to his sidearm.

Not swiftly enough. Charley turned the .44 Colt on the outlaw and emptied it into the man's chest. Noah collapsed to his knees, folded his arms across his torso, and stared blankly at the man he knew had killed him.

Charley stared back. "He who lives by the sword, Cousin," he said.

Noah's eyes glazed and he fell stiffly forward, thudding against the floor.

Charley slipped his gun back into his holster.

Chapter 18

Kathy struggled to her feet in the dark livery stable. She was dizzy, cold, and disoriented, and for a long time she stood in confusion about her whereabouts and what was causing the blasting noises outside. Then as her mind cleared she recalled what had happened, and that the noise was that of battle. The Murphy gang apparently had resumed its attack.

She became fearful and looked around her. But none of the outlaw gang's members were present, and she relaxed somewhat. She went to the open doorway of the livery, taking care to conceal herself, and looked out into the street.

The saloon was devastated, much of the wall gone and the ceiling collapsed. But the bodies strewing the street seemed to be some of Murphy's gang members. They appeared dead.

Yet the battle was continuing, the gunfire as heavy as before. Kathy was confused. If so many of the Murphy gang were wiped out, as it appeared, then who could be fighting?

Who but the people of Dry Creek themselves? She looked and saw it was so.

She drew back into the darkness of the livery, amazed and angry. Apparently Rand's division of the town had reached its apex and had broken into open battle. Kathy felt guilty as she thought of how the lies she had spread for Rand had added to the division. But she never could have imagined then that it would come to this.

Rand could not be allowed to get away with this. He had to be stopped. He had taken Sarah as a hostage to ensure his safe escape from Dry Creek, so Kathy knew that any move to stop him would have to happen soon or he would be gone into the mountains. Once he escaped the town it would be unlikely that he would be found again.

She stepped back into the door of the livery and waited a moment, then exited and went toward the Lodgepole.

She heard a man cry out on top of the Lodgepole as she neared the building, then a heavy body fell to strike the earth just inches from where she was. She gasped and stepped back, pressing her hand to her heart. Then she noticed a .44 Colt still gripped in the man's hand and knelt down to pick it out of his grasp.

Across the street in the saloon Bo Myers had at last managed to crawl out from under the heavy beam that had held him pinned to the floor. He rubbed his head, wincing, feeling the large, raw knot there. His gun was lost somewhere under the rubble, but there were plenty of loose weapons about, dropped by wounded men or held in the hands of dead ones. He picked up a Henry from the floor and tried to focus his eyes enough to rejoin in the fighting.

He took aim at a figure on top of the log building across the street. The man in his sights was just drawing a bead on one of the men in the Mansfield Saloon when Bo fired. The young deputy was honestly surprised when his shot struck the man, for he had been very uncertain and wavering in his aim. He levered a new cartridge into the rifle chamber and waited for another target to appear.

He noticed a rifle muzzle probing out of the small window on the west end of the Lodgepole, and he squinted into the darkness of the window to try to make out who was firing the rifle. He thought that the shadowy face that was faintly visible looked like that of Rand, but he wasn't certain. He hadn't laid eyes on Rand since the beginning of the fight. It seemed the gambler was making himself as scarce as possible.

Bo aimed carefully at the small window. When he saw movement of the man behind it again, he fired, then lowered his weapon and stared into the small dark square.

No movement for a long time. Bo grinned. If that had been Rand in there, it wasn't likely he would cut another deck of cards ever again.

But suddenly the rifle muzzle poked out again, firing more steadily this time, as if the man at the trigger was angry. Bo ducked. It seemed his shooting wasn't as good as he had thought.

As the battle progressed he examined the

situation. With the men in and on the Lodgepole so well covered, the odds were that the fight would continue without substantial losses to Rand's side. Compared to Rand's gunmen, the men in the Mansfield Saloon were in a very poor situation. Though there was plenty of rubble in which to hide on the Mansfield side, Rand's men had a clearer field of fire and could afford to aim more carefully as they fought, while the men in the Mansfield could scarcely get off an effective shot at their enemies without exposing themselves dangerously for long, tense moments. And if the men in the Lodgepole had plenty of ammunition, their fewer numbers would be little disadvantage.

Bo fired a few more shots, but after a time he became discouraged. The fight wouldn't be won like this. It would take something big to stop Rand's men, who seemed determined to fight until the end. And well they might; to surrender would be to volunteer for execution.

Then Bo saw it—another bomb—lying half-buried in the slushy snow just outside the ruptured front of the saloon. Apparently the dampness of the ground had caused the fuse to fizzle out before reaching the powder.

But it would work, if only Bo could get to it.

But how? Bo looked at it, thinking of the satisfaction it would give him to throw it onto the roof of the Lodgepole. If only he could get to it, break off the moist and useless portion of the fuse, get a match to the remainder. . . .

It would be dangerous to attempt it. A man could get himself killed.

Despite that, Bo forced himself over the heap of rubble and toward the bottle. He didn't look around or pay attention to the gunfire that intensified from the Lodgepole. His only goal was to get his hands around that bottle, to have it safely in his grasp while he darted back toward the Mansfield.

His leg collapsed beneath him and blood ran down his pants leg. He pushed back up and continued, his hand groping for the bottle.

A bullet ripped through his left shoulder, sending a shiver of pain through his side. But even as he pitched forward he felt his fingers close around the bottle.

He rolled to one side and broke the water-soaked fuse off near the top of the bottle. Rifle slugs tore up the earth inches from him.

Had he not rolled, he would have been killed instantly.

His good hand gripped the bottle, and he forced his wounded arm to move just enough to dig for a box of matches in his pocket. He found it and pulled it out, wincing with pain. Another bullet ripped through his foot, and he tried not to faint.

He dropped the bottle to the crook of his elbow and held it there as he rolled once more. Again the maneuver saved him and slugs plowed the earth perilously close to him. But in the midst of it all he managed to get a match lit, and some reserve of strength gave him the power to rise as he touched the flaring match head to the short fuse.

He grasped the bottle in his right hand, raising it high above his head. He wished he could toss the bomb through the small window where Rand was hidden, but he knew he couldn't afford to risk missing the small opening.

Into his mind flashed the night that he had in a sense started it all by telling Rand the story about Charley and the hidden Murphy money, and for a moment, just as he tossed the bottle, he was grimly satisfied that what he was doing now would make it right again, even out the score.

Bo didn't hear the rending blast of the bottle, for he collapsed, unconscious, before the bottle exploded.

In the small shed behind the Lodgepole, Sarah Redding heard the blast. She jumped, startled, and wondered what had happened. She shivered in the darkness, fighting despair.

After a time it became unbearable to remain still, and she stood and began moving around the small hut. Dim light issued in through the small cracks between the upright logs. She went to the widest opening and peered through, trying to see what was happening at the Lodgepole.

Smoke issued from the roof of the building, though the walls were apparently undamaged. She couldn't see much through the small opening, but the sound of continuing gunfire let her know that the fight wasn't yet over. The sound of shooting intensified, then declined.

The hut's door swung open. Rand, disheveled and dirty, stood there. He gripped a pistol in his left hand. His right shoulder was torn and bleeding. There was a light about him; dawn was breaking.

"Move!" he commanded, no longer displaying his usual calm. "And don't make a sound."

Sarah obeyed, trembling. Rand moved his wounded arm and grabbed her weakly, leveling the pistol at her temple.

"I got two horses waiting over here," he said. "Go get on the mare. And if you do anything to make our presence known, I'll kill you!"

Rand had the air of a desperate man. His hurried actions and worried expression were those of someone with no time to spare. He glanced over his shoulder at the alleyway beside the Lodgepole. As he grasped Sarah's arm his hand was trembling.

He shoved her forward. She stumbled but managed to keep her balance. Rand glanced nervously over his shoulder once more, shoving her again.

"Where are we going?" she said.

"Away."

A man appeared in the alleyway. He raised his pistol and prepared to fire at Rand, but the gambler shoved Sarah between him and the man, stopping him from shooting. Rand's pistol came up and he fired; the man fell back against the wall, gripping a wounded forearm. Before Rand could send a fatal shot into him, the man backed off into the safety of the alley.

Rand pushed Sarah forward to where two horses, already saddled, stood waiting in a hidden clearing in a stand of spruce, where Rand had hidden them earlier. Sarah mounted a gray mare, and the gambler mounted a tan gelding, grunting with pain as he climbed up. He had a long gash in his shoulder, an injury inflicted by Bo Myers' earlier shot.

He clicked his tongue and gouged his heels into the flanks of his horse, which began moving forward. He led Sarah's mare.

No sooner had they moved out of the hidden clearing into the open area directly in back of the southern row of buildings on Dry Creek's main street than a female voice called out, "Stop, Rand. Stop or I'll shoot you."

The gambler turned. Kathy Denning stood gripping a .44 with both hands. The weapon was aimed at Rand's chest.

Rand glared at the woman for a moment, then calmed, and the same deceptive, smooth air that usually hung about him returned. He smiled.

"Kathy, what are you doing? You know you won't pull that trigger."

"I will if you move."

Rand slumped in his saddle, studying Kathy. Then his hand whipped to his holster and drew out the pistol that hung there. But instead of leveling it on Kathy he aimed the muzzle at Sarah, clicking back the hammer and holding it with his thumb while his finger squeezed the trigger.

"Shoot, then. But you know as soon as my thumb lets up on this hammer Mrs. Redding will be dead. Do you want that on your conscience?"

Slowly Kathy lowered the pistol, then let it drop to her side. Rand smiled. Kathy looked at him with loathing.

"Thank you, Kathy. Now we'll be bothered with you no more." He swung up his pistol and fired a shot. She cried out, her feet kicking out from under her as the bullet knocked her down. Sarah screamed as Kathy fell; Rand laughed.

His laugh stopped suddenly when he turned to look squarely into the muzzle of Charley's pistol. The marshal approached in the growing light. The sun cast a bright ray over the eastern horizon, and it glimmered on Charley's pistol. Rand flashed a smile.

"Hello, Marshal. Looks like you caught me." The gambler's finger moved almost imperceptibly on the trigger of his pistol. Charley noticed.

"I wouldn't, Rand. I'll blow you out of that saddle."

"Now, Marshal, you don't think I would be such a fool as to . . ." The gambler dropped suddenly from his saddle, lunging for Sarah as he did so. He dragged her from her saddle and landed nimbly on his feet with an agility that took Charley by surprise. Then he jammed the gun against her throat, grinning in triumph at the marshal.

"Drop that gun or I'll kill her," he snarled.

Charley's eyes went cold as he stared at Rand. He did not break his gaze from the gambler's eyes as he raised his pistol. Rand's smile wavered, then faded, and he pushed the barrel of his pistol hard into Sarah's throat.

"I swear, I'll kill her!"

Charley fired one shot. It was sufficient. Rand took the bullet in the forehead, and he was dead before his body struck the ground. Sarah stood as if frozen for a moment, then rushed toward Charley, throwing her arms around him. Charley put one arm around her and let the other drop to his side, the pistol dangling in his hand.

Chapter 19

Kathy wasn't as badly wounded as Dr. Hopkins first thought. He took the bullet from her shoulder and confined her to bed. Charley came to see her while the doctor was still there. He waited patiently until the consumptive and very weary old man was finished with her, then sat down beside her bed.

Kathy wouldn't look at him. She turned her head the other way. Charley could tell her emotions were on edge.

"I'm glad you're all right, Kathy," he said. "I worried for you."

"You shouldn't have," she said. "You ought not speak to me, after all I did."

"It's over. Rand would have found a way to do what he did with or without you. I never knew he hated me so much." He paused. "I need to ask you something about Sarah. How did she get into a position to be taken by Rand?"

"She went to turn herself over to Noah Murphy, but Rand caught her first."

"She did what?"

Kathy repeated what she had said. Charley frowned. "Why would she . . ." He stopped, then patted Kathy's hand. "I'll be back to see you," he said.

He left the house and walked back toward the main street. Charley walked down the center of the street. People milled around him, cleaning up rubble, pieces of the barricade. The bodies already had been collected. Charley walked wearily, listening to the sound of weeping that the wind carried from open windows or from backrooms where women knelt over the bodies of fallen husbands and sons.

No one spoke to Charley as he passed; all seemed lost in their own thoughts, not noticing anything or anyone else. Their expressions ranged from benign to tormented. Charley passed the place where Bo had fallen and felt something like sand in his throat. Bo still lived, but he was badly hurt.

Not worth it. He believed now it had all been a mistake. He should have found some alternative to the violence—but he had never anticipated anything as bad as this. Maybe he hadn't been able to fully imagine what the siege of a town would be like.

Charley reached to the badge on his shirt. Without looking at it he unpinned it with one hand and tossed it into the dirt. No more. He was through.

He glanced at the Lodgepole. Rand's smoking saloon stood dark and solemn as a bad dream. Charley figured they would raze the place, wipe it out like the sad reminder it would be as long as it stood. He would do it himself if he planned to stay around. But he didn't.

Charley pondered Rand's hatred of him. Not being a grudge-holder himself, Charley had trouble coming to grips with Rand's motivations. He had known Rand had disliked him, and had held little respect for law—but Rand had obviously arranged for his men to try to kill Charley during the battle. Charley figured Rand had recruited most, maybe all of them independently for the same job; certainly Rand's men had seemed quick to take up battle against their fellow townsmen, as if all had something to fear.

"Charley!"

Charley turned. Dr. Hopkins was approaching. He looked a decade older than he had a week ago. Charley waited for him to catch up, and for him to finish his predictable spell of painful coughing once he had.

"Charley, I . . ." The doctor stopped and looked around. He laughed mirthlessly. "You know, I thought I had something to

209

say about all this. But there is nothing worth saying."

"That's right. Except maybe thanks to you for the work you've done. How many have we lost?"

"Too many. I quit keeping count when it got too much to bear. Where's your badge?"

"Gone."

"Lost it?"

"Threw it away."

Dr. Hopkins paused somberly. He coughed again, then said, "Oh."

The two walked together. "Where will you go?"

"Don't know. Anywhere but Dry Creek."

"With Sarah?"

Charley did not answer. He veered to the left and walked away.

When she saw Charley alone near the livery, Sarah smiled and ran to him. She threw her arms around his neck and kissed him.

"I was so afraid I'd lose you," she said.

Charley looked into her eyes. He was not smiling. She lost her own smile and pulled back.

"What?" she asked.

Charley remained silent.

"Charley, what's wrong?"

Charley took a deep breath. "You're a hard one to understand, Sarah. A mix of nobility and greed."

Sarah looked shocked. She let go of him and backed away. "What are you saying?"

"Why did you go looking for Noah Murphy?"

"I thought maybe if I turned myself over to him he would stop the fighting."

"What good would that have done? If surrendering to Noah would have stopped this thing, I'd have done it myself right at the beginning. But it wouldn't have helped, because I don't know where the money is. Noah would have beat me, burned me, cut on me until he was satisfied I really didn't know, and then he would have killed me and attacked the town anyway. Same would have held for you. Didn't you know that?"

"Of course I did."

"So you're telling me you were ready to turn yourself over for torture just so Noah could find out you didn't have the information he wanted?"

"I thought maybe he would just listen and go away—"

"Nonsense. You're not that foolish, and you're not that brave. You've got your share of grit, I know, but I don't believe you would

211

willingly hand yourself to Murphy unless you knew you could tell him what he wanted to hear. After all, he'd have no cause to hurt you then."

Sarah's face reddened. "Are you implying that—"

"That you know where Willy Murphy hid the money? You bet I am. Why else would you have taken the risk you did, unless you knew it really wasn't risk at all? That's the strange thing about you, Sarah—you had the decency to at least try to sacrifice your little secret to Murphy once you saw how bad all this was. That's worth some praise, I suppose, but blasted little. How many dead men did it take to tip the scales for you? Why didn't you just tell where the money was in the beginning?"

Sarah looked like she was about to cry—whether from shame or anger, Charley could not tell. Suddenly she burst out, "You want to know why I didn't tell at the beginning? Because the money was hope! Do you know the loneliness I've had out there alone since John died? Do you know how hard it is to make it on your own, wondering if there's to be enough food for the winter, or if you can keep enough wood cut to make sure you don't freeze to death? Willy Murphy said where the money was while he was raving in his sleep. Nobody but me was there to hear. Sure, maybe I should have said something, but I couldn't. I knew that with that money, I could build a real life for myself . . . and one for you." She paused, then drew nearer. Her voice lowered. "I still can, Charley. We'll go out and get the money together, leave this place . . . no one will ever know."

"You think I could live with you, knowing what you did?"

Sarah bristled. "What I did was risk my life to try to tell Noah Murphy where the money was! I was ready to give it up! It wasn't my fault Rand got to me before I could reach Noah!"

"I suppose it wasn't. But I consider it your fault that Bo Myers may die, like so many others already have. I consider it a fault of yours that you only developed your moral fortitude after innocent folks were killed because of you."

Tears came; Sarah drew back her hand and swung a hard slap at Charley. He caught her forearm and blocked the slap.

"You're going to tell me where the money is hidden," Charley said. "Then I'm going to ride out of town, pick it up, and take it in to Denver where it belongs. And you won't say a word about it."

Sarah sneered at him. "You plan to take it for yourself!"

"Nope. It's a temptation, but I'm a man sworn to law. I'll live by what I swore to."

"Aren't you the righteous one!" she declared sarcastically.

"Not righteous. Just somebody who figures his life is worth more than a bag of stolen money." Charley glanced over his shoulder at the wounded town of Dry Creek. "And the lives of others, too."

Sarah seemed to break. "I didn't mean to do wrong. I didn't."

Charley's throat grew tight. "Maybe you didn't. I'll grant you that much. But you did do wrong, Sarah. You lied from the beginning, you led me to think you were something you weren't . . . and you let people die when a word from you would have saved them."

She forced herself to stop crying. Wiping her eyes, she said, "So what happens to me now?"

Charley sighed. He looked up and rubbed the back of his neck. He was more tired than he could ever recall being before.

"I figure I might turn in that money and

maybe sometime later send back the word that Sarah Redding knew where it was all along but didn't tell. I don't know what folks here will do once they learn that."

Sarah grew afraid. "You can't do that!"

"Maybe I won't, then. Maybe I'll just let you live here among these folks you betrayed. You can watch them heal from this —and it'll take a long time—and when they start smiling again you can think back on what they've been through and what you had to do with it, and see if you can live with that." He changed his tone. "Maybe sometime or another you'll even think of what we might have had with each other."

Her lip trembled. "I'll have to leave Dry Creek, then, no matter what. What will I do?"

"I suppose that's your problem."

"I hate you."

"I figure you don't. I figure it's yourself you really hate."

She glared at him. "I'll never tell you where that money is. And if you leave, the people will believe you just went to get that money for yourself."

"Then I guess it's up to me to talk to the good folk of Dry Creek about you right now.

I think they could convince you to talk; they can come with me and you to retrieve that cash to make sure we stay honest. Then I suppose the widows of some of these men can find some ways to deal with you. We can handle this like Injuns, with the squaws avenging their dead warriors. It could get right savage for you." He turned from her and walked back toward the heart of the town. He felt her gaze upon him for half a dozen steps.

"You enjoy this, don't you!" she called after him.

He turned. "I don't. God knows I don't feel like I'll ever enjoy anything again."

He turned again and kept walking. She watched nervously.

"Wait," she said. "Come back."

Another night came and then another morning. Alone in the forest, Charley hefted the bag from a space beneath the rocks. Just where Sarah had said it would be. It was made of leather, filled with money, and stamped with the name of a Denver bank. He brushed the moisture and dirt from the bag and put it beneath his arm.

His horse stood waiting on the trail a

hundred yards away, a loaded packhorse strung behind it. It was just past dawn; Charley had ridden out in the night so as not to be seen. He didn't want anyone to follow him here, and follow him someone surely would have, for there were still those who believed he had known all along where the money was. No one would have believed he planned to take the money back where it came from—and even though he was nearly broke and had no idea what lay ahead for him, that was exactly what he would do. Maybe he could claim some kind of reward.

It was just one more reason to leave Dry Creek. He could list plenty of others: a dead mother, a town wounded beyond full healing, trusts destroyed, hopes shattered, mistakes made, and a love lost.

The last one was what cinched it for Charley. He would never be able to think of Dry Creek now, much less live in it, without thinking of Sarah Redding and missing her. Not Sarah as she had been the last time he had talked to her, but Sarah as she had seemed to be when he had declared his love for her in the marshal's office in Dry Creek.

At least he would carry away the memory of that one good hour before Dry Creek's bad night. It wasn't much to take with him, but a man had to be satisfied with what he had.

He stashed the money in his leather saddle bag, mounted up, and rode.